The Life We Chose

Dre

Edited by: Abman Glaster

ISBN 978-0-615-43283-0

THE LIFE WE CHOSE by: Andre Cooper

STREET DREAMZ PUBLICATIONS
P. O. Box 258
Chester, PA 19013

www.streetdreamzpublications.com

Dedication

In memory of my time lost behind bars.

Acknowledgments

First and foremost, All Praises and Thanks are due to Allah. I would like to thank Allah for the countless blessings He gives me day in and out.

I would like to thank the best woman ever in my life that has always been there for me no matter what the situation called for. Mom, I love you more than words could explain.

I would like to thank my Dad. I love you, Old Man. Even though we lived totally different lives I always respected you more than anything.

I would like to shout-out my boys, Lil Dre and Tahiaj. Remember that I love y'all and both of y'all are the reason why I continue to go hard.

I would like to thank my Grandpops (Arthur & James), Grandmoms (Sandra & Florence), Aunt Tonia, Mark, A.J., Aunt Judy, Aunt Fennia, Aunt Jane, Uncle Anthony(love you bul), Cousin Tone, Pubs, Mike-Mike, Rock, T-Money, Shake, Butt-Butt, and James(The real Lil Nigga). To my brother Lil Kevin (don't give up on ya dream bro.) To my sister's, Brittany (keep ya head up out there), Kierstein, Gee-Gee and Shonda (You grew up on me so fast. I love you.)

I would like to thank my man Shy, Kontal (It's been a long time Ockie), V.A. Black -aka- Tenio (Love you bul), Marqui (West Philly), Hot Rod (West Philly), Lonnie Dawson (Saleem), Philly Ty (Is this illest nigga from Germantown), Kasim (Zulu Nation), Big Al (Germantown finest), James Hairston (Alim, I finally got this jawn done.), Derrick (D-ware), Sage, Lil Ant, Mar-Key (I hope I spelled it right), Crazy ass Jihad (My North Philly man), Miller (Detroit), Tameia (What's up stranger), Natalie (Get at me!), Shawanna (The real hustler's wife.

Hang in there wit my peoples), Pebbles (Thanks for the encouraging letters), Somaj (Be easy out there youngbul), Bear, Shaheem, Lil Roe, Rockie, Lil Bird, Jayanna, D-Rock, Abu Bakr (My Main man from Chi-Town), Beanz (Petersburgh), La'nees (I still love ya), and Abman Glaster (Chew).

To my men, La-La (love you bul), EC -aka- Eastwood (Hold ya head, Ockie. Remember that they can't never count them niggas from the Gardens out.), Paris (It's been a long time, homz), Park, Scrap, and Scobby.

To Erika, the mother of my son. Let's forget the past, so we can have a better future.

To Jay & Tate my brothers from another mother, although we share the same father (The Streetz). This shit'll be over in no time. I love y'all and that's from the heart.

Last but not least to my sister's, Keyana & Ayanna, the biggest supporters of everything I do; y'all both know how deep my love run for y'all.

Rest in Peace to my peoples, Cousin Brad – aka – Buttons, Cousin Cory (Atl), Hass, Relly Rock (Rock Star); and Nakira Grable, the mother of my son; I truly miss you.

To everybody else, if I forgot you, maybe you forgot about me.

Salaam Alaikum

Chapter 1

Summer of 1999

Sitting in front of Evon's house, I got a call from Young'in, who had anger in his voice. Right away, I knew something was wrong.

"What's up?" I inquired.

"You around?"

"Why?" I asked sitting up in my seat.

"Yo, Nieem, Face just got hit up real bad."

"What!" I shouted causing Evon to jump. "Where at?"

"Up the way, hurry up Nieem, it don't look too good for him."

"Nieem what's wrong?" Evon questioned just as he disconnected the call. From the look on my face it couldn't be good. "Talk to me baby." She said grabbing my arm.

"Listen, I got to go." From the tone of my voice, plus the cold look on my face, Evon knew not to press me. Instead she just sighed. "Look, I'll call you later."

◆　　◆　　◆

When I pulled up on the scene, minutes later, my stomach began to knot up at the sight of all the saddened faces on the dozens of people standing around. Fuck, I knew it was over. Hopping out of my truck, I moved through the crowd, heading over to the white Buick rental car that was crashed into a gate, with the driver's door open. Through the back window, I could see Face laying across the passenger seat.

The driver's door had two holes and the driver's window had been shot out. I could see glass on Face's lap and on the floor. It looked like he got hit a couple times in the chest, because his white t-shirt was full of blood. Emotionally, I was fucked up; Although, I couldn't express it. Not now, at least. The only thing I could think of was revenge.

"Step back, step back, away from the crime scene son." said the Police, whose voice snapped me back to the moment.

"Fuck you, and cover my mutha fuckin' peoples up, you bitch ass nigga."

"Step back, before we lock your ass up." He shot back.

"Nieem, chill man you drawing (bringing heat). I know you fucked up about this shit, but you got to use your head," said Young'in.

I thought to myself, damn bul right. Right then, I pulled out my cell phone to call my Mom to let her know what happened.

She picked up on the first ring. "Hey Mom," I said with anger and sadness in my voice.

"Yes, what's wrong baby? Why you sound like that?"

"Face, just got shot up at..."

"Nieem, stop playing!" She said with disbelief...

"Mom, I'm dead serious. He at the top of Culhane Street."

It was silence on the other end of the phone. "Mom?"

2

"Oh my God, I'll call you back."

The line went dead. "Damn!"

Now I got to find out who done this shit. I know for sure somebody out here seen something. Nothing happens around here, without somebody seeing shit go down.

◆　　◆　　◆

Minutes later I pulled around on my block and got out of the truck. My squad was standing out there, like ten deep. All of these niggas had that brick look (mean face expression). Everybody loved Face and they knew he was my heart.

I hopped out of my all black Cadillac Escalade with limo tint, dressed in a White Sox fitted hat, white t-shirt and black Dickie pants that hung perfectly over my black quarter top Chuckas (timberland boots).

My truck was way bigger than my 5'7, one hundred and fifty pound frame. You wouldn't think such a little man would be driving, such a big toy.

The Escalade didn't have any special rims on it. I kept the regular Caddie rims and wheels on it.

From the street lights, you could see the glow from my beard which I just got treated earlier in the day. Young'in then walking over, and the first to speak. "Nieem, what's up homz, you aight?"

"Naw, I got to find out who did this shit."

"We already got word. Tiz, bitch seen the whole thing from her window, but she on some shit like don't put her name in nothing because she ain't trying to be next." said Young'in.

"Man, fuck that bitch. Where Tiz at?" I replied, growing a bit angry.

"Around the corner at her spot."

"Come on and take this ride with me."

On the way around to her spot, Young'in told me that a bul from up the way was driving pass the nigga when he was running down the street about to shoot Face up. "So, why didn't the bul run the nigga over?"

"He thought it was a nigga from up here playing around and shit."

"So, who was the bul that seen this nigga with the mask on running down the street?"

"That nigga O. The one, I told you was soft as shit. That strange ass mutha fuck'a I'll hit that nigga ass up for you, if you want me too." Young'in said, meaning every word of it.

"Not right now. We got to get this other nigga first. Face was my mutha fuckin'man. We was like brother's." I pulled up to the house, and I hit the horn.

"There go that nigga Tiz looking out of the window."

Tiz was a big black husky nigga. He walked out of the house dressed in a yellow Polo t-shirt, a pair of regular denim, Polo baggy shorts, with a pair of wheat ankle length Timbs with cushion around the ankle. Tiz came up to my window, "Nieem, what's up?"

"You tell me?"

"Nieem, that bitch in there scared as shit. She don't want to talk to nobody at all. She just said that Rell from over the bridge in Feltonville did that shit. She seen him walk down the street, first without the mask on, looking at Face in the car the whole time. But, she thought Face must've been sleep, or something, because the bul Rell just kept looking and walking real slow. Then, she said when Rell got to the top of the block, he turned around and threw the mask on, and ran up on the driver side and started shooting. After that, he ran through the little alleyway on the side of her house," Tiz finally ended.

"Did she say who was outside when this happened?" I asked.

"Naw."

"Go back in the house and ask her did O ride pass when the nigga Rell was coming down the street."

"Aight, hold up."

"Young'in, this nigga Rell got balls doing that shit. I'ma blow this nigga top off when I catch him."

"You know, he fuck with the bitch Roz from around the corner in Park Terrace. I know exactly where she live." said Young'in.

Tiz came back out of the house and said "Nieem, she said yeah, O rode pass and he slowed down for a minute, then kept on going."

"Aight Ock, give Shonda this stack and tell her I said good looking, and to keep her mouth closed about this shit."

"Nieem, I'm going to let her know, but the babe too scared to talk to anybody about this shit. She is in there crying right now as we speak," said Tiz.

"I'm going to holla at you later Tiz." I said then pulled away from the curb. "Young'in, I hope that bitch stay cool and don't go to the police, before I get to his ass."

"I know that's right." said Young'in.

"Let's take a ride past Roz spot."

We rode around to Park Terrace, which was only around the corner from Boyle St.

"Look Nieem, there go that nigga Rell right there."

"Yeah, I see him. Look at him staring at the truck. Just watch his movements. He don't know, we know yet."

"The nigga on to us though, because he ain't trying to walk down the street yet to his car." said Young'in.

"This nigga think he got all the sense. He rocked Face, then hurried up to Roz house, so, just in case somebody did see him. He probably got her backing his play, saying he couldn't have did the shit because he was with her.

Yeah, I'm going to play it smart too. I'm not going to kill his ass right here and now, because I can't let my emotions do the thinking for me. Nigga's always get caught up like that and get booked."

"Nieem, the nigga on to us for real. Look, how he watching us." said Young'in with a bit more excitement in his voice.

"I know, that's why I'm going to give him a pass tonight. No shoot-outs right now. The way already hot."

"Yeah Nieem, you right." Young'in chipped in.

"Listen, I'm going to call it a night. Where you want to get dropped off at?" I said a bit frustrated.

"Drop me off on the block. I got to shut it down and all of that shit. Plus, I got this chick I'm supposed to get wit later on tonight. We shooting down to Atlantic City.

Nieem, why don't you come with us, just to clear your mind and shit. She got a sister that is bad as shit, and I know you can fuck tonight," Young'in said matter of factly.

We pulled up to the block, and I told him "naw man I'm good. I'll holla at you tomorrow. Make sure you up early tomorrow nigga and be on point while y'all out here tonight. Rell might try some sneaky shit and come back and hit you niggas up."

"Nieem, I stay strapped. I wish that nigga would show his face out here."

"Aight, Young'in I'ma get wit you."

As, Young'in got out of the truck I called my Mom back to see what was up. She answered on the first ring sounding relieved to hear my voice. "Nieem!"

"Yeah Ma?"

"Where you at?"

"I'm about to leave from up the Gardens now."

"Please baby, go in the house. Please. We all just left from up there. They finally took his body to the morgue. I was the one who identified him.

Baby I'm going to have nightmares of him laying there across that seat with all that blood over his face.

Please Nieem, go in the house and please don't get involved in this. Let the cops deal with it." She pleaded, "please baby, I know you two was like brothers but let them handle it."

"Mom, we still don't know who did this to him."

"Nieem, I hope it wasn't over no drugs or something stupid."

"Me too Mom. Well I'm going in, did Mira call you?"

"She said to call her as soon as possible."

"Is she in the house already?"

"Yes."

"Aight then, I'm going to call you tomorrow Mom."

"I love you."

"I love you too." I said then disconnected.

◆ ◆ ◆

Jumping on the highway I dreaded the long-ass ride I had ahead of me to get home to Delaware. Picking up my phone from the passenger seat I dialed my home number.

"Hello," Mira answered.

"What's up sunshine?"

"Nothing. You alright? I heard about what happened to Face." She responded in a sad tone.

"Yeah, I'm good."

"Where are you?" She inquired.

I could hear the concern in her voice. "I'm on my way home."

"Okay, I'm going to wait up for you."

"You don't have to. Go ahead and get some sleep."

"You sure?"

"Yup."

"Okay, I love you."

"I love you too sweetheart." After hanging up, I pulled into the first rest area and parked then shed a tear for my brother.

Chapter 2

"Nieem, good morning baby. I didn't mean to wake you up with all that noise I was making." said Mira.

"Naw I was just laying here watching you."

"Why didn't you wake me up last night when you came in?" She asked.

"Because, you was looking so beautiful sleeping. Plus, I knew you had a long day at school yesterday, and needed your rest."

"Well, I'm not going to school today. I told your Mom I was going to stop by and help the family out with all the arrangements and all of that type of stuff, just to show a little support. How are you feeling though?"

"I'm good"

"You hungry?" said Mira.

"Not really, come here and give me a kiss. I love you Mira." I said kissing her neck.

"I love you too. I got some good news to tell you too."

"What?"

"I'm pregnant."

"Yeah?"

"Yeah," said Mira.

"How many weeks?" I asked.

"3 weeks."

"When did you find out?"

"Yesterday, I was trying to stay up last night to tell you, but I feel asleep."

"Come here baby... Damn you smell good."

"Ooh, boy don't start nothing you can't finish."

"Shut up girl, you know I finish everything I start."

"Ooh, baby I like it when you kiss there. Damn Nieem don't rip my panties."

Mira's pussy was extremely wet and feeling so good. That's when I rolled her over and put both legs on my shoulders, taking nice and long strokes with my tongue. "Umm baby, open your legs wider. Let me tongue fuck you... Damn this pussy taste good."

"Nieem, let me turn around and suck ya dick, while you eat it. You know that's our favorite."

"Come on, anything for my baby. Damn girl, that feels so good."

"Ooh Nieem, oooh baby, keep it right there. Don't stop. Please don't stop. Oooh pleeease, let me get on top. Let me get on my dick..."

"Mira, this pussy so wet." I said feeling her juices running down my leg.

"Yeah, this that pregnant pussy nigga."

"Damn, I feel all that juice running down my leg."

"Nigga, this pussy is, wet as shit for you. This what I had waiting for you last night."

That's when she told me, "stop baby", and pulled my dick out of her pussy and start sucking it again. Looking dead in my eyes, she asked, "how do you feel baby?" I couldn't even talk, because I started cumming. When Mira seen that, she started deep throating it, trying to get every last bit of the cumm.

Just as I finished cumming, my cell phone start ringing... "Let me answer that baby, it might be important." I said reaching for my phone off the bedside nightstand "Yo".

"What's up Nieem?" Young'in voice barked.

"What's up homz?"

"Where you at?"

"In the spot. Why what's good?"

"Naw, I was just calling to see what's up. You ain't call me this morning, so I wanted to know if you wanted the block open, or not." Young'in stated.

"Go ahead and open the jawn up. I'll be down there a little later. I got some other shit to take care of first. Who all out there?"

"All the youngbuls; Shaheed and Sahih out here too. They said get wit them or do you want me too put them on the phone now?"

"Naw, tell them I'm going to make a run. I'll be up there a little later."

"Bet," said Young'in.

I hung up and faced Mira, who didn't hesitate with her line of questioning. "What was that shit about wit Face?"

"I don't know."

"Yeah right, nigga don't lie to me." She said folding her arms and frowning.

"I ain't lying."

"Yes you are Nieem. I been around you too long not to know when you are lying or telling the truth. I know you're not going to tell me, but baby just please be safe out there."

"I'm going to try my best... Let me go get in this shower, though. I got some shit to take care of. Did my uncle call here this morning?"

"No, but your Mom did and she said call her, and that he was looking for you anyway.

Nieem, you know he ain't calling here. That nigga don't play no damn phones at all. What he so paranoid about?" Mira asked suspiciously.

"Unc, from the old school. He don't believe in that talking business over the phone."

"I guess that's where you get it from, huh?"

I just laughed and shook my head, "let me get in this shower girl."

A half-hour later I was finished with my shower and getting dressed. After kissing Mira goodbye, I told her to tell my Mom I'll be past there later.

"Oh, tell her to holla at Aunt Trina, and to tell her that Face is getting buried as a Muslim. Not none of that Christian shit.

He is Muslim, even though he been on some bull shit lately."

"I'll tell her, but you know how they are." Mira said just as I exited the house.

Hopping into my truck, I couldn't help but notice how nice and sunny it was.

You could tell summer was about to touch. First thing on my agenda is to go and see what's up with my Uncle. I know he's going to be mad as shit. Unc told me to look after Face and I let him down.

Along the drive, my mind drifted back to when me and Face was coming up together. We both grew up in good houses, according to the hood standard, with both parents in our lives; Even though they weren't together, they both were active in our upbringing. Face lived with his Mom and seen his Dad off and on every other weekend.

Me, on the other hand, I lived with my Mom until middle school. That's when I moved with my Dad in Delaware, leaving my Mom, Grandmom and two sisters behind in Chester, but I came back to see them every weekend. The reason I had to move was because of getting in too much trouble at school-fighting and normal little boy shit from growing up in a tense environment, around nothing but drugs, and seeing murders and shoot-outs everyday didn't help my behavior any either.

Every weekend I came back, me and Face would get like a whole ounce of weed and go to these girls house up the Highland Gardens, but we called it the Gardens for short or Killa Hill, which was on the Westside of Chester. Killa Hill, heavy with drugs and murders and you had to be on point walking the streets, no matter what time of day it was.

The girls' mom was on drugs, so she was never there. Which meant, we could get high and fuck the shit out of them and just chill.

Uncle Saleem would always come looking for us. He knew when me and Face got together, there's no telling what the hell we would get into.

Of course, we would duck the shit out of him, running from this spot to that spot, so he wouldn't catch us all high on that weed.

Face's real name was Raheem, but we all called him Face as a kid, because on one particular day, he was fighting with another youngbul and he was beating Face ass, so he grabbed a bottle and broke it on the ground and hit him in the face with it. That put a long cut on the youngbul, and after that, the name Face just stuck wit him.

Everybody said he looked like he could have been 2Pac's twin, size and all. He was like 4 yrs older than me, so I always looked up to him.

Face was always in the streets. By his Dad seeing him every now and then and Aunt Trina working he was free to run the streets like he wanted. Face was the first one to start hustling and the first to show me a gun he had bought from a junkie.

Uncle Saleem tried to keep us out of the streets but he was too busy out there himself. And how could he tell us not to sell drugs when, he riding around dropping shit off and picking money up with us in the car. I always felt that, that was Unc's way of showing us the ropes.

Sometimes, we would be at his crib and I would be at the door listening to him fuck a bitch and watching out for Face who would be taking some powder(cocaine) out of the bag. He never took a lot, where as though he would notice; just enough for him to make some money to buy our weed.

So one weekend I went down my Mom's crib. I put Face down wit what I was trying to do. Now, mind you, Face is already hustling and he tells me, "cuz, I'm tired of this".

"What" I asked naively.

"I'm tired of us going behind Unc back and doing shit. I'm going to holla at him about putting me on." And a week later Face started a block down the street from the Old heads, cutting their money off, and they knew Face was selling Unc's work, and they didn't want any problems with Saleem.

Soon after, I joined the team and we was off to the races. Then, we found out we both had a passion for something greater-robbing niggas. On one of our first jobs, we came off with $12,000. From this we inherited "The Young Gunz". I remember that shit like it was yesterday!

Chapter 3

After leaving Mira, I was headed to Unc's spot. My Uncle Saleem was a major nigga but he was real low key, though.

Unc was slim, 180 pounds, stood 5'10 and didn't look a day older than 40. He didn't wear a big beard like most Muslims, only because it wouldn't grow. Instead, he wore it shadowed and sported a baldy, which stayed covered by a kuffi.

Unc wasn't flashy, like most major niggas I know. He don't have all them dumb ass cars and shit. This nigga be investing all his shit in to houses and apartment buildings and shit like that.

He tell me all the time to stop wasting all that change on a bunch of bull shit. I tell him that I'm young and don't give a fuck and I'll make that shit back. Plus, I love to front. These niggas out here be trying they best to keep up with a nigga.

I grab a new Mercedes Benz, they breaking their necks trying to get one. The difference between me and them is my shit is paid for. Them niggas hustling to pay the car note.

Some of these lame ass niggas still riding around in BMW X5's and shit. What they didn't listen to Jay-Z, when he said we don't ride X5's, we give 'em to baby mommas.

Man, I heard that shit and the same day I brought Mira one.

Saleem was always trying to pull my coat on shit. I know, I'm about to hear it now that Face got rocked. Me and Face was like his son's. His biological sons, Jihad and Lil Saleem got booked for a body, when they were 14. They killed these niggas trying to run down on them while they was at some girls spot. My Uncle was messed up over that for awhile, but they both made out okay on the case by only getting juvenile life. They'll be home when they turn 21. They should touch in like 2 yrs. I wonder did he tell them about Face yet?

Pulling up in front of Unc's spot I thought, let me park in the back of the store, he always says that whenever I'm driving my Escalade or the Benz don't park in front of the store drawing.

His spot is a Halal restaurant. The food is good as shit, but it's high as a bitch. It's called Ameer's after one of his sons that died at birth. As I'm parking I see one of the sisters that work in the store, in the back throwing some trash away.

"As-Salaam-Alaikum, Amina."

"Wa-Alaikum-As-Salaam, Nieem."

"Saleem in there?"

"Yeah."

"Tell him I'm coming in."

When, you walk in the restaurant it's beautiful. It got a section where, if you want to sit down and eat, you can. There are big Persian rugs covering the floor where the counter is, from which you can see all the food being prepared. I walked in to see my Uncle sitting at a table by himself. "Unc, what's up?"

"You tell me?" said Saleem with a serious look in his eyes.

"I found out who killed Face already," I said taking a seat.

"I knew you would. Who done it?"

"The bul Rell"

"Rell?" said Saleem, sounding surprised.

"Yeah!"

"Rell that be coming down to the Masjid all the time? He done lost his fucking mind." Saleem said, almost in shock.

"That's what I said."

"Well it's only one place for niggas like him," said Saleem staring me directly in the eyes.

"I know."

Getting up, Unc nodded for me to follow him to the back, where he had the work (100 pounds of weed and 15 birds of powder) already packaged and ready to go. Rell's name didn't even come up anymore. We both know what had to be done and I would definitely handle my business.

◆　　◆　　◆

Now, hitting the corner on 9th street and turning on to Highland Avenue, I'm looking and thinking about this fucking ran down ass neighborhood I grew up in. Damn, I'm glad my Mom moved out of this shit hole. Look at it abandon houses everywhere. Mind you, this place used to be a military base back in the days. The houses were beautiful and kids could play outside. Eventually, the military families moved out and was replaced by whites, then came the blacks.

That was back in my Uncle Saleem days. I remember Unc telling me that they used to fight the white boys everyday up here. It wasn't too long before they started selling cocaine on the street corners to those same white boys. Then, from there it was on.

Soon as you turn off of Highland Avenue, you go up this big hill and then that's where all the action is; right in the middle of the neighborhood.

The Gardens is located right on the side of I95 highway, so when you either are going to Philly from Delaware or from Delaware to Philly you see the exit Highland Ave you can look right up and see the whole hood.

The Gardens been known for getting money thru the years because of this highway. Most of the customers are coming from down Delaware to grab.

Now, of course, with drugs comes a lot of killings, and Highland Gardens became known as a little killing field. Niggas from Philly and Delaware be shook coming thru here. Even niggas in the city don't like coming through this jawn.

Seeing niggas getting killed and shit like that became normal to me. I just thought it was part of the game. So, people in the hood gave the Gardens the name Killa Hill and the thing about us up here, ain't no snitching, we take care of our own problems.

Now Park Terrace is an apartment complex in back of Killa Hill. It's two ways in. The place is old and ran down but they try to make it look good by planting bushes in front of the apartments. Which are double units, with one apartment down stairs and one upstairs. To get in the apartment upstairs, you have to go in thru the side of the building, and to get in the downstairs apartment you enter from the front of the building.

At night it be real dark and spooky around here. That's because niggas be shooting the lights out on the telephone poles. That's why a lot of niggas be getting caught slipping around here. Plus, that's how niggas be getting money.

Park Terrace is part of the Gardens according to all of us around here. It's infested with a lot of hood rats and junkies. I even got a little DL spot around here, where I keep my work and fuck my little bitches.

Niggas think I live here, but they got me fucked up. I wouldn't dare live around these crazy ass niggas.

I parked the truck, grabbed the bags with my left hand and had a 40 cal. in the other, then headed towards the door. My apartment didn't really have nothing in it. Except, an all black two-piece leather furniture set. I walked to one of my bedrooms. The other one didn't have shit in it, except boxes of shoes and clothes laying on the floor with a mattress near the window. I went in there and headed straight to the safe in my closet, and put the work up. I decided to separate everything later, then hit Khalil up; my man from Delaware.

When I moved wit my Dad, he was one of the first niggas I started to fuck wit. He was a short nigga between 5'6 to 5'7. You could compare his look and style to Nas the rapper. He was a fly little nigga. I dug his style.

Back in the day, we used to be in school smoking in the bathrooms and shit, and the white boys used to always come up to me and ask me did I have any of that Chester weed. I used to sell them little J's, doubling the price on them. I knew that they couldn't get none of this weed nowhere in Delaware. So, I put two and two together and holla'd at Khalil and asked him did he want to start getting some money, instead of smoking all this weed up. He said 'damn right'. I told him I had to holla at my peoples from the city and see what's up first, but for sure it was on. And the rest is history.

As I'm leaving my apartment, I see my man Shaheed riding past in his all white Denali sitting on some factory chrome rims.

Shaheed pulled over and jumped out. He and his brother Sahih, these two niggas are like brothers to me. We all grew up in Killa Hill together.

Shaheed and Sahih both started hustling on Boyle Street back in the day. That's the street they lived on growing up. Now mind you, Shaheed is 6 ft 2 inches and his brother is 6 ft. They both got like a light brown skin complexion. People say Shaheed looks a lot like Charles Barkley. Sahih, to me, looked more like the basketball player Tim Duncan. He thought he played like him too.

People say they are twins, but they are a year apart and to me them niggas don't look nothing alike. Maybe it's because I grew up with them all my life.

We all fuck with my Uncle Saleem. I got the block jumping with that weed and powder and they got the block jumping with that Boy (Heroin).

Plus, us three, we been thru a lot of shit together from fucking bitches, doing robberies to shoot-outs with niggas, we done it all.

"What's up Homz?" I said.

"Ah man, I'm good. What's up with you?" Shaheed responded giving me dap.

"I was just about to swing thru the block. I had to stop past the spot first. Where Sahih at?"

"He around the corner on Boyle. You holla at Saleem today?"

"Yeah, he told me to tell you and Sahih to stop by Ameer's."

"We going to go holla at him later, when we shut the spot down for the day." said Shaheed.

"Any money coming out there today?"

"It's kind of slow, because police been riding around trying to question people about that shit last night. Plus, I seen that nigga Rell walk past the block today, looking like he was wearing a bullet proof vest, or something, underneath his t-shirt.

Young'in told me and Sahih last night the conversation you niggas had about him. You know my brother fucking his peoples. She fucked up over Sahih too. That nigga hate that shit, he be trying to give Sahih the brick and everything." Shaheed ended.

"Shaheed, I'm about to go over to the block and see what's up with Sahih and Young'in. What you about to do?"

"I'm looking for this youngbul around here that owe me some paper, that's all."

"Aight then, I'm going to get with you on the block."

Damn, should I walk thru the alleyway up to the block instead of driving because all of these damn police is out here? I can't afford to get pulled over with this 40 cal. on me.

I'm going to go ahead and walk. I need to study my get away route from around here anyway, because I know this is where I'm going to catch that nigga Rell, coming out of that bitch Roz house down the street; I thought then went off about my business.

Chapter 4

Now, I hit Boyle Street, where we got the work on top of the corner of Boyle and Culhane Street. On this narrow block is a bunch of small family houses, with mostly section 8 people living in them.

Coming out of the path, money looked like it was flowing as usual; it was like fifteen customers out there, not including the junkies that were lined up on side of the yard, on the corner. Young'in out here running the block and got all the youngbuls serving fiends.

"Young'in, what's up?" I asked.

"Nie, where you coming from?"

"Around the spot."

"Why you walking?" Young'in asked.

"Shaheed told me police was running around like crazy."

"Man, fuck them cops. They know who the fuck we are, the fucking Young Gunz." Young'in said cockily.

That's why I fuck wit this young crazy nigga. He was down for whatever and whenever "How much work you got left?"

"Like 9 ounces, but I got Tiz coming in like a half, to grab that." said Young'in.

"You not going to break it down on the block?"

"This nigga keep on begging me to front him the shit, talking bout he trying to come up."

"How?" I asked.

"He said he got this bul from Chi-Chester trying to buy a half of jawn (18 ounces), so he going to re-rock the 9 ounces and bring it back to a half of brick and give me 10 stacks off of it."

"Oh, aight then. Where Sahih at?"

"Down the street talking to one of his youngbuls. So Nieem," Young'in said before I could walk off.

"What's up Ock?"

"You got more work?" Young'in asked.

"Yeah, I just scored. I'm going to take you around the spot, so we can break everything down.

Yo, let me go holla at Sahih, then we're going to walk back around my spot." I said.

"Yo, Sahih," I yelled down the street to get his attention. He turned around and started walking towards me. When he got close enough, we shook hands and I asked "What's up player?"

"I'm good. What's up wit you?... Everything aight wit the fame?" Sahih shot back.

"Yeah, I'm about to go back around my Mom spot to see what's up with everybody. They all gathered around there, putting everything together for Face."

"Ae Nieem, I told you we should have been rocked the bul Rell. I think it's our fault that Face got rocked. When that nigga approached Face about that shit that Roz did. The way he walked away and just had that look on his face made me think that he was up to some sneaky shit. Plus, when me and that nigga had words over that girl he got a baby by. Y'all niggas told me to chill that I was over reacting. Now look, if we had hit that nigga up then, we wouldn't be all fucked up in the head about Face," said Sahih.

"I just seen Shaheed around the corner looking for some youngbul." I said switching the subject.

"Man, I told Shaheed fuck that youngbul that we was going to send Young'in around there to deal with him. So, Nieem what you about to get in to? You staying out here with us today or what?" asked Sahih.

"Naw, I got to make a couple of moves first."

"When, y'all going to bury Face?"

"Tomorrow, hopefully. That's where I'm about to go," I said.

"Where down to the Masjid?"

"Yeah."

"Nieem you know that Aunt Trina and your Mom ain't going for that." Sahih said knowing my family was.

"I know, but I'm going to try to put the press on them about it, though. Right now, I'm about to walk back around my apartment and break this shit down I just got from Saleem. He told me to tell you and Shaheed to get at him too."

"I'm going to get with him later on. Where he at today anyway?"

"Ameer's."

"I'm hungry as shit too. Soon as Shaheed come back we are going to slide past there."

"Young'in come on man, walk around here with me to break this shit down.

Ae Sahih, I'm going to holla at you later. Be on point out this jawn," I said.

"Young'in you coming back?" Sahih asked him.

"In probably like an hour, I'll be back," He responded.

"Aight. Yo, if y'all see Shaheed tell him to come and grab me from around here.

If I ain't out here I'm going to be in my Pop's crib," said Sahih.

"Tiz came while you was down there talking to Sahih," said Young'in.

"Aight then, let's go. Plus, let's walk thru the other path way, up there towards Roz apartments," I ordered.

"Ae Nieem, I know how you niggas always telling me to chill and stay out of the way and shit like that and always asking me why I stay strapped all the time. For the same reason that happened last night. Man, if I was that nigga O riding down the street and seen a nigga running with a mask, a gun in his hand, I would've ran his ass over, then jumped out and hit him the fuck up. Then I would've just dealt wit whoever later. You feel me?" said Young'in.

"Young'in, I feel you, but everybody ain't built like us because I would've done the same thing," I answered.

While we are talking, me and Young'in are walking thru the alleyway, up here we call it the path. We got six of them in the Gardens. How the streets are designed in the hood, they are all shaped in a U, and at the end of the U, which is on the side of the houses of the six of them, you got big alleyways that we use to get to the next block, without having to walk on the main street.

There are two alleyways that lead to Park Terrace. It's only a big gate separating the two. We keep a hole in the gates to walk back and forth. Plus, just in case somebody has to run from the police.

"That's where he will be expecting us to get him at. So, that spot, we can't use. Even though it's a good spot," I said.

We continued to walk down the street. I started fucking wit Young'in about this junkie, we saw. She keep calling him for some work, he say, but I think he probably hit her on the low before, because she keep talking all freaky to him.

Suddenly Young'in started "Nieem, we should just break in Rell's crib when nobody's there and wait for him."

"Naw what if he comes in with her and the kids. Don't get it fucked up, I want to kill her too, but not no kids and shit like that. I don't need that type of drama in my life. Niggas go to jail for shit like that. Police try hard as shit to solve them type of cases. Plus, the nigga going to be on point for something like that I know I would be."

Finally, when we both get in the door to my spot Young'in asked, "so what's the plan old head?"

"Let me think it out, before I put you on. Take a seat. Let me grab that coke for you," I said and came right back. "Here go 5 bricks. Break these all down to 20's. How did you bag up the last 5?"

"Off of every brick I bagged up 40 stacks worth of 20's and with all the shorts and shit we took, we made 175 stacks. I gave you 140 and took 30 for myself; paid all the workers with the remaining 5 stacks," said Young'in.

"Bet, keep it just like that," I said.

"Ae, Nieem, you know I love you to death Ockie. I'll take a bullet for you nigga. This money shit ain't bout nothing. Death before Dishonor, old head," said Young'in.

"Yeah, I feel you Ock. Here take these jawns and do what you do. I got to go past my Mom spot and stop down the Masjid."

"Tell, Muhammad I send my greetings to him."

"I will."

"I'm out homz, I'll hit you up a little later," Young'in said, then headed out the door.

"Aight."

Young'in left and I'm thinking to myself, let me get on out of here. Damn before I forget, let me put this alarm on. I turned the alarm on, checked the safe again and turned the lights out and bounced.

Outside I jumped in my truck and hit the music. Jay-Hova started blasting thru the system. Young'in just said some real shit to me. Homz said he would take a bullet for me. Young'in already proved to me that he was a fuckin' soldier. A couple of years ago, me and him got chased by police. We both had hammers on us. Instead of both of us getting caught, Young'in stopped and tackled the police, so I could get away. He got caught with my 9mm he had on him and a bullet proof vest. He was on probation, so they sent him up state for 4yrs. We used to write each other all the time and I used to send the nigga some change whenever he needed it. Even though he already had older brother's getting money around Killa Hill I treated him like my own.

Young'in is my mutha fuckin' man. I could never second guess his loyalty to me. So, when he came home I put him in a brand new all white Yukon, with 35 percent tint and gave him my best block to run.

While he was gone, me, Shaheed and Sahih start getting major money. We, was young and was just hustling our asses off. We wasn't fucking with all them different girls, just our main jawns and we wasn't going to no clubs or buying no expensive cars and jewelry. All, we was doing was trying to eat. Nothing else mattered. That's when Young'in came home and we all looked out for him. Plus, don't get it fucked up, Young'in was on some bull-shit before he got booked. He was part of the reason why they call niggas from Boyle Street the 'Young Gunz', but the bul was shooting shit up like it wasn't nothing. You look at one of us wrong, the nigga was going to hit ya ass up. He a short nigga 5'6 probably, with brown skin and kind of husky from being up state. He'd remind you of

Styles P from the L.O.X., a little bit. I know if I'm not on point, he is and he definitely is going to squeeze.

Driving past my Mom house, I see Mira silver BMW X5 parked on the corner of the block. I just told her ass the other day about parking her shit all the way at the end of the block. She ain't going to be happy until one of these hood niggas grab her dumb ass. Niggas be trying to eat out here on these streets. She know what type of shit I be into and she still don't be on point. She lucky she pregnant now because I would have played a trick on her ass and had a nigga snatch her just so she could see how real this shit is. Bet she'd stop taking shit for granted then.

I didn't find a parking space on the crowded block, so I parked across the street in the A-Plus gas station. I got out of the truck and walked across the main street. The house on the outside had a regular family house look. When you are walking up to the door, if the blinds are open, you could see the whole living room, because the windows in the front of the house are big, and from the inside you could see the traffic outside, so she kept them open in the day time and closed them at night. The house was in good shape and the block was a mix of whites and blacks.

I get in the house and see my Mom first. She is a short beautiful lady, who wore her hair in a wet-set, her long silky black hair; matched her brown skin complexion. She looked very young. In a couple of months she would be turning thirty-five years old.

My Mom had me when she was only fifteen. My Dad was also the same age.

"Mom, what's up?"

"Hey baby. How you been holding up?" She asked, then kissed me on the cheek.

"I'm good, where Aunt Trina at?"

"Sitting back at the dining room table."

"Did y'all decide where to bury him at?" I asked.

"She was waiting to talk to you."

"Where Mira at?"

"Upstairs in the bedroom. Keisha and Shay in their room and grandmom went out to make a run," My Mom said.

"Let me go holla at Aunt Trina."

Mira came down the steps and called me. "Nieem, come here for a second."

I walked over to her and said, "give me a kiss baby. How my little boy doing in there?"

"Boy, I'm only 3 weeks. I don't know. How you know it ain't a little girl?" Mira said joking.

"You tell my Mom and them yet?"

"No, I was waiting for you to come in here so I could tell them... Come here Nieem let me whisper something in your ear."

"What?"

"Nieem, my pussy so wet right now. Let's kick your sisters out the room and get it in right quick, pleeease." Mira begged.

"Damn this baby turning you into a little freak, huh?" I said.

"No boy, you know this pussy stays wet for you. As soon as I feel your presence this pussy start to leaking. Come on, let's go up stairs!"

"Naw, calm down girl. Let me talk to my Aunt first."

When, I walked away from Mira. I saw my Aunt Trina in the dining room. She is a beautiful lady. Aunt Trina was really my Mom's first cousin, but I still called her my aunt. She was an older lady with a little bit of gray in her hair with a dark brown skin complexion. Aunt Trina stood no taller than 5'3.

"Hey Auntie, how you doing?"

"All of this is driving me crazy Nieem. Why they had to kill my baby Raheem? Why? Why?" said Aunt Trina in a sad voice that you could barely hear.

"So, what did y'all decide? I want to bury him as a Muslim." I told her.

"Well, I want all of his friends and stuff to view him first. So, we are going to have a viewing and then we can have a Janazah (Islamic funeral) with just the family attending," said Aunt Trina trying to sound strong.

"Aight. I'm going to holla at the Imam (Religious leader of Muslims). Make sure you call the funeral hall and set up a viewing for tomorrow from 9 to 3, because we have to put his body in the ground as soon as possible. So, get on top of that now, while I go holla at Imam Muhammad and let him know what's going on. Aunt Trina, how much money you need to pay for the viewing or anything else?"

"Saleem already gave me everything I need, plus more. I'm okay for now," said Aunt Trina.

"What about his kids. Did y'all tell them and his baby Mommas about everything?" I asked.

"Yes, we did."

"Aight, I'm going to go talk to the Imam. Mira I got to make a couple of more stops. Don't stay here too long. I want your ass out before dark. Call me when you leave. Mom I'm leaving. I got to go to the Masjid to get everything moving."

"Baby, be safe out there." My Mom said.

"I'll try to."

Chapter 5

"As-Salaam-Alaikum."

"Wa-Alaikum-As-Salaam, Brother Nieem. How have you been? I haven't seen you around here in a long time," said Muhammad.

"Muhammad, I been busy."

"Too busy to worship Allah?" He shot back.

"Naw, not like that. Just caught up in this dunya (worldly life) all crazy."

"I heard about Raheem!"

"Yeah, that's what I came to holla at you about. We need you to perform a Janazah tomorrow around the Asr (mid-day) prayer."

"I just got off the phone with Saleem. He told me all about it. I would love to perform the Janazah for the family," said Muhammad.

"How much is it going to cost?"

"I'm doing it for the sake of Allah. All you have to do is pay for the material needed. In-sha Allah (God-willing)."

"Well here goes 200 hundred for the material."

"Nieem tell all the sisters that's coming, to dress appropriately. Make sure their hair is covered and no tight fitting clothes. In-sha Allah."

"Salaam-Alaikum Muhammad. I'll see you tomorrow. In-sha Allah. Oh yeah they are going to bring the body by here at 3:00 p.m. In-sha Allah."

"Wa-Alaikum-As-Salaam, Brother Nieem."

After, meeting with Imam Muhammad I needed to go drop this weed off down to my buls in Delaware; Khalil and R. I met R from playing basketball down the park on 24th Street. He lived right there on the corner house. R, real name was Rico. He was a tall nigga like 6 ft., with a brown skin complexion. He talked with a scratchy voice. He had the park on lock selling weed, when we was young.

Now, Khalil got the whole block to his self on 2-4. He got a gang of youngbuls out there running it for him. Yesterday morning he told me, he needed some more work. So I got to drop 3 bricks and 50 pounds off to him.

R, on the other hand, don't hustle on no corners or have no blocks. He get money off the customers thru his phone, and sell only weed. R told me that it was the safest way to get money, because the Feds be riding around all the drug spots snapping pictures of people out there moving work.

Before I make my way down Delaware I had to slide past my spot around Park Terrace and grab the work for them. When I pulled up it was a bunch of hood ratz out front of the apartment across the street from my spot. It was Janelle and her crew. I damn near fucked all of them. They were all strippers. And some bad little broads at that. I got out of the truck and paid them bitches no mind.

After getting everything I needed out of the apartment I jumped on the highway heading to Delaware. You got to be careful on I95 with these Delaware State Troopers. As I'm getting off the exit, I slowed down and drove like I had some sense.

I'm headed to see Khalil first. Market Street was the best way to take to 24th Street. As I'm riding down Market I'm thinking to myself, 'I hope he got all the money around that he owe me. If not, fuck it I know he good for it. Khalil always held me down when I needed him and I sure did need him right now. Plus he owe me one, for doing him a favor awhile back.'

Last year around Christmas, I put Khalil and R on this girl from Philly that I use to fuck around with. She was getting a lot of money by driving drugs from Texas all the way back to Philly. She was doing this for her baby brother and she had been doing this for quite awhile, so she was up at this time.

I met her through a girl that I've known from Chester, but who hung in Philly. The girl in Chester was the one who put me down on how she was getting money because she was messing around with the Philly girl's baby brother. After getting plugged in with her, we was going out for awhile and having fun together, but my plan the whole time was to line her ass up. She got so comfortable around me that she took me to her Condo in Camden, New Jersey. The place was crazy. You could tell she was doing some major shit. It was a two bedroom Condo. When you walk in the spot, she had plush white carpet with customized Italian white leather furniture, that consisted of a love seat and matching Ottoman with a sofa two feet longer than the standard size. She didn't have any television in the front room. It was very nice and neat. All she had was pictures of her family members and one large portrait of herself, done in black and white. When she took me there, I knew for sure that this was where all the money was at or at least some. So, I put a plan together with Khalil and R.

During this time, Khalil was just coming home from a 3 year bid and ain't have shit. R was getting money, but he was my man, so I had to put him down with this one. I told them to come and lay on us and grab me and the girl to make it look good. Everything went good, and we got 300 hundred stacks out of the Condo. This was the biggest sting all of us ever had. R started a business called 'Cotton Candy' with his share. He got into the business of party promoting. Khalil on the other hand flooded 2-4 with work from his share.

Ever since I looked out for him on that sting, he told me that if I needed him for anything, he would hold me down, and now I'm going to see if he is a man of his word.

I pulled up on 2-4 and saw a bunch of youngbuls out on the block that I don't know. I stopped anyway and rolled down the window. "Ae youngbul, where Khalil at?"

"He just walked down the street... Matter of fact, there he go right there." said the youngbul.

"Good looking," I said and drove off.

Khalil saw me and walked up on the truck. "What's good wit you Nieem?"

"Ah man, your hand is the best hand. I came down here to bring that work you wanted," I told him.

"Why you didn't call first, so I could've brought your money out wit me?"

"Naw, if you ain't got it around it's cool. Listen aight, I need to holla at you about something."

"About what?" Khalil said sounding concerned.

"My peoples just got hit up last night."

"Who?" Khalil asked a bit hyper.

"My cousin Face." I said.

"Damn, sorry to hear that. Did y'all find out who done it yet?"

"Yeah."

36

"Is he dead yet?"

"Naw."

"Why not?" Khalil frowned his face.

"Because I need you to put in that work for me."

"Who is it?"

"This bul name Rell." I said.

"I got you Ock... Just tell me when and where!" said Khalil.

"The nigga do a lot of walking, around my way."

"Even after he killed ya peoples, this nigga still walking around like shit sweet. Yeah, the nigga really think he ruff." Khalil said shaking his head in disbelief, "I got you Nieem. When you want it done?"

"Friday"

"Who's going to pick me up after I hit him up?"

"Young'in."

"Young'in?" asked Khalil kind of wearily.

"Why, you want somebody else to pick you up?"

"Naw, Young'in cool"

"Ae, Khalil I got to be on the scene, my name already be in too much bull shit as it is. My peoples be on my ass about my name popping up in different shit."

"Yeah, I feel you Ockie. You don't have to explain to me... So, what you bring down here for me?"

"1 brought the 3 bricks and 50 pounds you wanted. I need 20 thousand a piece each for the bricks and 700 hundred each for the weed."

After Khalil gathered all the work together and put it in a City Blue bag I had in the truck, I told him that I would get wit him on Friday around 9:30pm and to bring a gun with him.

I rode around the corner and pulled in front of R mom's spot and started blowing the horn, he looked out the window and said, "hold up Nieem for second. Park, I'll be right down."

R made his way out of the house and got into the truck and said "Nieem, what's good wit you? You drawing on me when you be blowing that horn in front of my spot. Niggas around here know that you bringing that work down to me. Plus, my promoting thing jumping in the city right now. I don't want nobody thinking that I be holding no money or weed in my spot." R said, looking a little pissed off.

"Ae calm down. These niggas too soft around here to be running up in anybody spot."

"What's up wit you though, Nieem?"

"Ah man, I been going through it today."

"What happened?" R inquired, generously.

"I don't know if you remember him or not, but my peoples named Face got killed last night."

"Damn, sorry to hear about that."

"But anyway though, I got those 50 pounds you wanted."

"Yeah good looking. I got a sell for them waiting right now. Here go the 35 stacks from the last work you gave me. What you about to get into?"

"I'm about to go get wit my young jawn."

"Where at, down here?"

"Naw, back in Chester."

"Well, I'm going to let you go ahead and get wit her. Holla at me in a couple days. I might have something lined up for us." R said like it was a for sure thing.

"Aight" He got of the truck and went back inside the house while I made my way back to the highway. I was also debating with myself about whether to take this money he just gave me to my house in Newark now, while I'm down here, or just wait. I decided to go ahead and take it with me, because I was going straight to my apartment.

After finishing everything I had to do for the day, it was still early, so I wanted to spend some time with my baby girl

Evon. I have been putting her on hold lately. I've known her since we both was in elementary school. We were always friends nothing more. When we started messing with each other it was on the low, because she had a boyfriend at the time. Things just happened out of the blue.

One day me and my man Roe, was going to get something to eat; Roe was my man from way back. We came up thru the trenches together. He and a couple other niggas named T-Bone and Brody had a block called the Cutt-Off and at times people called their spot the Circle of Death, it was around the corner from my block. It was all still in the Gardens; we was just getting money at different spots. Roe, was a short and stocky light skin nigga with a big neck and gut. He weighed like 250 with a 5'8 frame.

Roe was fucking Evon friend Niesha. Niesha reminded you of Naomi Campbell to the tee. She was a real freak, too. Niggas in the hood nick-named her 'the machine.'

It was an inside joke to all of us who knew her. Roe was trying to take Niesha to get something to eat, but she wasn't going if Evon wasn't, so Roe asked me to go with them.

I went along with the plan. After we ate, Roe and Niesha left us and went to his house. During the whole time we were eating, me and Evon were flirting with each other. So I started putting the press on her. One thing lead to another and before you know it, we were in the Hilton fucking like crazy.

By Evon being from up the Highland Gardens and us growing up together, she already knew everything about me and that Young Gunz shit. She also knew about my girl Mira and understood all that.

Evon was a street girl and sexy, too, so it was easy for me to put her under the wing. She was a sexy red-bone like 5'7 130 pounds. She got nice big titties with a slim waist. Her walk is so crazy, it is sorta run-way type with a thuggish twist to it.

Ever since that night in the Hilton, me and Evon been sneaking around seeing each other. It has been two weeks since that day in the Hilton and I will admit that she got me fucked up right now. If it wasn't for me loving Mira the way I do, Evon definitely would be my number one.

While still on the highway I grabbed my dutch out of the astray, lit it, then turned the music up. Biggie's song came on "Niggas bleed just like us. Picture ah nigga hiding my life in that man hands, while he just deciding. Niggas bleed just like us. Picture ah nigga shook, we can both pull burners and make the mutha fuckin' beef cook." That nigga Big talking that real street shit. Niggas definitely bleed just like us.

Now, I'm getting off the Highland Ave. exit at Chester. My peoples live right off that exit, so as I'm riding past the house I still see Mira's truck out front of the house. As, I pulled in the Gardens, which is only a couple of blocks from my peoples house I see it's packed outside. Everybody and their mother is out.

I saw my man Roe, so I slowed, and rolled down the window. "What's up nigga."

"Nieem, what's good wit you?" Roe asked.

"Ah man, I'm chilling." I said dapping fist with him.

"Yo, I heard what happened last night... It's all around the City that Rell done that shit." said Roe.

"Yeah?"

"Yeah Ock, so let me know if you need me, because you know I fucked wit Face hard."

"Naw man, I got everything under control. You know I be about my business."

"No doubt, but I got to check anyway, feel me?"

"I feel you, did you see Evon around here?" I asked switching topics.

"She just walked up the street. I think she was walking home, or up to the block."

"Oh, aight. Let me hurry up and catch her. I'm going to holla at you later, Ock."

"Aight."

Pulling off, I seen Evon walking with that mean thuggish run-way type walk she got, looking pretty as ever. She had on a sun dress and a pair of white stilettos looking tall and sexy, hiding behind a pair of black Gucci glasses.

Pulling up on her, Biggie was still banging in the truck. I honked the horn, two times, and she turned around standing there with her sexy stance. Evon saw it was me and started smiling walking towards the truck.

I asked "what are you doing walking around here? You killing that dress, too."

"I was walking around on Boyle to see if I saw you out there... Oh baby, I miss you. Give me a kiss." Evon said leaning in the window.

"Come on get in the truck."

"Where we going?" She asked, while hopping in.

"Around my spot. Why you got something to do?"

"Naw, I just wanted to know, and why didn't you call me back?"

"I forgot. I had to make a couple of moves." I said, while pulling off. We drove around the corner to Park Terrace talking the whole time. When I'm pulling up to apartment, I saw this bitch ass nigga Rell walking down the street. I thought to myself, 'damn, Shaheed was right the nigga do got a bullet proof vest on. This bitch ass nigga don't even know that he got less than 48 hrs to live.'

Evon seen the look on my face and asked me, "Nieem you aight?"

"Yeah, why you say that?" I asked, trying to keep my composure.

"Because, everything was cool until you seen Rell... Everybody said he was the one that killed Face last night."

"Naw, it wasn't him... I already found out who killed Face."

"Yeah."

"So, whoever told you that shit, tell them to get the fucking story right. You think I'm going to let a nigga like Rell walk around breathing, while my cuz is not? Hell No." I demanded.

"Damn, I'm sorry. Don't kill the messenger," said Evon.

"Naw baby, it ain't like that, it's just that people will fuck shit up and make a story up and get an innocent person killed."

"I feel you," Evon shot back.

"Come on sweetie, let's go inside," I said, grabbing her hand.

We both stepped in the crib, and I'm just looking at Evon walking. I told her, "Evon you look good as shit in that dress."

"This the one you bought me" she replied.

"I know. What you got on under that?"

"My Gucci all white lace set."

"Come here baby, let me take that dress off."

"Be gentle... You know how you get, start ripping clothes and stuff."

"Shut up girl, and give me a kiss... Umm, you smell so good. What's that, peaches you got on?"

"Yup."

"Do you taste like it too?" I asked.

"Maybe!" Evon said, in a real sensual tone.

That's, when I grabbed her ass and lifted her up, and while kissing her, she wrapped her legs around my waist. Evon got one arm around my neck and with the other hand she grabbed my pants, trying to unzip them. When she finally was able to unzip them, they immediately dropped to the ground. With the same hand she then grabbed my tool, massaging it up and down. That's when I moved her panties to the side and she stuck my tool in that wet cuchie.

I just kept whispering to her how good that cuchie is.

"Go harder, harder baby." She begged.

I went harder and harder.

"Umm baby that feels gooood," she bloated, in ecstasy.

I got both hands on her ass, while she was pumping back too. Damn, her pussy was so wet and feeling so good.

Right when I start moaning she asked me "Umm baby you about to cum?"

"Oooh, baby." I moaned unable to talk at the moment.

That's when I let her down and she started sucking my tool, giving me long deep strokes. It was feeling so good, I couldn't contain myself. I started cumming long and hard, and she was catching everything. After I finished cumming, we both went and got in the shower.

Chapter 6

Face's janazah (funeral) was on Friday, at 1:00pm. Imam Muhammad lead the funeral prayer. He stood there in his all white Islamic thobe, with a white kuffi on. The Masjid was packed, it was over a hundred people in attendance, paying respect to Face.

We had the brothers on the sharif (security) staff, on guard, just in case anybody tried to come thru and shoot the place up. The Masjid had a big green Islamic rug in it with a picture of the Haraam (The Holy Masjid in Mecca), which covered the whole floor. There were no pictures inside the place. It had a big wash room, where you offered your wudu (the washing of the hands and feet to purify yourself to pray). Also, it had some rooms for Muslims that didn't have a place to live, due to them being poor, or just coming home from jail, with no place to go.

The prayer was a two unit prayer. Me, Saleem and the rest of my crew that was Muslim, stood in the first row to pray first with the Imam and offered our two unit of prayer to Allah(God). I personally asked Allah to forgive Face for his sins in this life, and any other things he done wrong. Hopefully, the supplications of all these Muslims would help him get into Paradise.

After we all was done, we let the rest of the brothers line up and pray to Allah for him. The women, and everybody else that wasn't Muslim stood all the way in the back. Face had already been given a viewing at the Church. We only did that, so all of the non-Muslims could see his body. When you get buried as a Muslim, you get covered in an all white Yemeni cloth. Face was wrapped from head to toe. Aunt Trina and the rest of the family was crying in the back of the Masjid with the rest of the people. After everybody was done praying over his body, we all went to the Islamic burial plot that the Masjid has. It wasn't too far from the Masjid. It only took us like ten minutes to get there.

Imam Muhammad already had the hole dug for him. A couple of other brothers helped Muhammad put Face inside the earth, with his body pointing to the Holy city of Mecca, where Muslims all over the world pray towards.

When I was there watching Muhammad put Face in the earth I was offering another supplication to Allah for Face. Right then and there I knew it was time to handle that beef with Rell. My whole family was fucked up over Face getting killed.

Tonight, had to be the night; Face's death would be revenged. I just hoped Allah, would forgive me for taking another Muslim's life.

Chapter 7

It was Friday, around 9 o'clock, and everything was in place. I had Khalil in the car with me to explain everything, then I asked him "Khalil you ready to do this shit?"

"Let's get it."

"Now, Young'in just called me and told me that the bul Rell is walking up Boyle.

So I'm going to give you this walkie-talkie right here, and the rented car right there by the tree. I left the keys in the ignition, so after you hit him, you can jump straight in the rental and be on your way.

When I see him walk past this street right here I'm going to hit the stress button on it. Soon as I hit the button, that mean he's right there and you can hit him."

"Nieem, how many people outside up there?" asked Khalil.

"It's packed up there that's why I brought this mask for you to wear; here it go." I said, passing it over. "But look, when I pull off, I want you to walk up to that abandoned house near the corner and wait for the signal on the walkie. When you hear the signal, put the mask on and just run straight out and hit him up. I know I already showed you a picture of him, but he got a black T-shirt on with a white kuffie. Also the rental car got New York tags on it that are stolen. Just in case somebody might see you get in it and write the tag number down. So when you get back to Delaware, take the tags off and put the real ones back on. I left the real tags in the back of the seat. Oh, before I forget. Here go that Mack 11 you wanted."

"Aight, I'm good." said Khalil.

"I'll be standing out there watching everything," I said.

"Aight." Khalil replied.

"I'm going to go ahead and park up on the block." I said, and while pulling off, I'm thinking to myself 'man I hope he don't fuck this up and miss the nigga, because then he will know that the hit came from me.' It was good timing, Evon was walking down the block. Let me hurry up and jump out and talk to her, while Khalil hit this nigga. I pulled over and got out the truck. "Hey baby, what's up wit you?" I said.

"Nothing, I was just walking around here to see what you was doing?" said Evon.

"I'm just out here watching the block right now, making sure everything running right," I responded.

As I'm telling her that I see the nigga Rell walking on the other side of the street, I reached in my pocket and hit the button on the walkie twice.

No sooner than after I hit it, I saw Khalil run from behind the house with a mask on. All the youngbuls start running from the corner. Boom, Boom, Boom, Boom, Boom, Boom, Boom, Boom, Boom, Boom... I grabbed Evon and threw her to the ground, faking the whole time. I looked up to see Khalil jumping over top of Rell, and giving him two more in the head. Then, he ran down the street to the rental car.

Twenty seconds later, I saw the rental car hit the corner. By that time, everybody was running over there to the body. Then I heard one noisy mutha fucka saying, "that's him in the black car with the NY tags; I seen him get in the car at the end of the corner, after the shooting."

I'm glad I told him to put a mask on, or else I would have had to kill this noisy mutha fucka. I turned and looked at Evon and said "Evon, Evon, you aight?" I asked.

She said, "I'm cool. Y'all crazy around this bitch."

"Why you say that?"

"I'm tired of all this shit up here. Every other day people are either getting shot or killed around this bitch."

"I know."

"Who was it that got shot?" She asked.

"I don't know. Go see who it was!" I said.

She walked over and said "Nieem, oh shit it's Rell!"

"Damn, that's fucked up... I wonder who the fuck did that shit to him," I said, trying to sound surprised. When I start hearing the police sirens I told Evon "Ae, I'm gone. I ain't staying here with all these cops coming around. I'm going to call you later." As I'm saying this Young'in is walking up the street calling me.

"Nieem come on Shaheed and Sahih in the truck waiting down the street."

Me and Young'in walked towards the truck they were in, and Young'in said "Nieem that was a clean one."

"Yeah, this is only the beginning," I said.

We then got in the truck with them. The first thing Sha heed said was, "I see you took care of that."

"No doubt. They don't call us the Young Gunz for nothing. I wanted to do it around Park Terrace, but Young'in called me and told me he was walking past this way, so I had to get him. Fuck it though, that shit right there is going to send a message to everybody saying that don't fuck with them niggas from the Young Gunz. They 'bout their business for real," I said with the straight face.

"Yeah, you right." said Shaheed.

"But we are going to have to shut the block down for a lit-tle while, until shit blow over." said Sahih.

"Fuck that shit, we getting money. We ain't shutting shit down," I told them.

That's when Shaheed said, "Saleem going to be pissed bout this shit happening on the block."

"Let me deal with my Uncle."

"So what you niggas trying to get into tonight, because we got to get off the block, for at least tonight?" said Young'in.

We all went to Atlantic City to gamble and fuck a couple of them China dolls that work in them massage parlors. We was celebrating for Face.

Chapter 8

Boom, Boom, Boom, Boom...came the thunderous knock, which caused me to jump out of my sleep, in a panic. Man who the fuck is this banging on my door like that? I know it ain't the FEDS, because they would've been kicked my shit in. 'Let me look out the window first,' I thought. I saw it was Sahih, let me hurry up an open the door; it must be important.

"Sahih, what's up?"

"My bad for knocking so hard, but I had to get in here. You ain't going to believe what just happened around the store." He said taking deep breaths.

"What?"

"Me, the nigga Big Boy, and the young bul Little D was around the store gambling."

"Aight."

"And Big Boy was on some bull shit, trying to play a nigga about a point, so I snapped on him, because you know I ain't going for nothing."

"No doubt."

"So we start arguing, then the nigga swing a lazy ass right. He must'a forgot that I used to box back in the day, or something, because I dips that shit and straight pulled out my gun on the nigga, and just start shooting.

Then I ran through the bul Brian house, then on to Boyle and jumped in the car and came straight around here."

"Damn Sahih, where the gun and shit?"

"Right here. I need to get rid of the shit."

"Let me throw something on right quick." I took off to my room. Ten minutes later we were driving in my truck. All the while I'm thinking to myself, this nigga just did some crazy shit, but what the fuck, Big Boy would've done the same shit.

I just hope ain't nobody see Sahih do the shit.

"Who was at the store?" I asked.

"Like I told you, me, Lil D, Big Boy and it was a lot of bitches and shit in front of the store when we went down the alley and started to gamble."

"So they didn't know y'all was on the side of the store?"

"Naw, not that I know of," Sahih said, kind of unsure.

"Did Big Boy have a gun on him?"

"Damn right he had one. I seen the mutha fucka poking out on his side when he was shooting the dice. Come on Nie, you know I ain't on no nutt shit. I had to shoot that pussy, because if he would have connected with that right, then next he was going for the gun. He didn't go for the gun first because he know I had mine in my front pocket, so I beat him to the draw first," Sahih said confidently.

"Where Lil D at?"

"I told him to stay at the scene, to see who talk to the police or anything."

On our way to Philly, I threw his gun over the bridge in the river, then threw his clothes into a trash can, at a gas station.

After telling Sahih, he had to lay low for a minute, he told me he was going to chill with this new Philly girl he met. So I told him, "you ain't never told me about her."

"Young jawn look good as hell. She go to school at Temple University, studying to be a corporate lawyer. She like 5'5 100 pounds, and is Ethiopian. I took her to dinner and a movie a couple of times. She just got out of a relationship wit this major nigga from Philly. I think he from up North. I heard his name before. His name Huss. You heard of him?" Sahih asked.

"Naw."

"Well anyway I forgot to put y'all down on what she was telling me, because I was going to do some homework first on him."

"What she tell you?"

"Ock, I got her all drunk one night. We was in my spot up Philly drinking that Cris and she just started running off at the mouth about this nigga. Telling me how he be counting money in front of her. How many safes he got and about all the bitches he be cheating on her with. Now, mind you, shawty ain't no street girl, so she not evening on point about what she is doing and she don't get drunk like that. So the liquor is really talking for her.

The babe grew up in Mount Airy with a good family, her Pop's a doctor, and Mom's a dentist. So, that right there show you what type of girl she is. The babe is crying and everything talking about how she done fucking wit hustlers and all that. So when I start seeing her crying and all that I took full advantage of her. Telling her don't worry, I'm here to save you and protect you. I got her thinking that I work for a construction company and that I buy and sell houses.

Anyway, while I'm laying low I'm going to do some homework on this nigga Huss. Plus, to make things even better, young jawn woke up the next day and I told her how drunk she was and that she was crying. She told me that she don't remember none of that. I was just testing her to see if she remembered telling me about the nigga. Ae, Nieem I took a mental note that night about her. Never let her know shit about what I'm in too." Sahih ended.

"No doubt nigga. It sounds like we got to get on bul ass quick, before he start moving shit and stuff like that. Because I know I would after I leave a bitch alone that knew too much."

"You right, that's why I'm going to lay on the nigga to-night."

"Where he live at?"

"In Jersey, in them new houses they just put up over there," said Sahih.

"You want me to lay on him with you?"

"Naw, I got it. I need you and my brother to make sure everything is good up there on the block. When I'm ready to grab the nigga Huss, then I'll call you niggas."

"Where Shaheed at anyway?"

"He had to take his daughter school shopping, so he playing family man right now with the wife and kids at the mall."

"What mall he go to?"

"King of Prussia"

"Oh, aight."

After we got finished talking, and all of that, I turned the music up and he laid back in the seat. I did it because I know he wanted to clear his mind, after what he just did.

I just hope ain't nobody see my man hit that nigga. If so, I know we are going to have to get rid of all them fuckin' witnesses, because one thing about us, we ain't going down for no fuckin' bodies. No bull shit!

Chapter 9

After me and Sahih got finished taking care of everything I dropped him off at his spot. He told me to park his car that he left around my crib, and to take it to his Dad house on Boyle St. He told me his Philly girl was going to get him a rental car to ride in for awhile.

It hasn't even been two months and this is the third body to drop in the Gardens. My Uncle Saleem going to be mad as shit about this one. But shit, he got to understand that Big Boy asked for it.

Let me go ride past his store to put him on point about what the fuck happened and that Sahih is going to be laying low for a little and about this sting (robbery) that Sahih just put me down on.

♦　　♦　　♦

I walked in the spot, to see it wasn't crowded. Maybe because it's only 12:00 pm, it normally gets packed around 1 or 2.

"Salaam-Alaikum, Amina."

"Wa-Alaikum-As-Salaam, Nieem." the Muslima responded. "Where Saleem?"

"In the back. What you been up to Nieem?"

"Trying to get rich or die trying, sweet heart. That's all I been up to. I'm going to holla at you though, when I get finished in here wit my Uncle."

"Okay" Amina said with a bright smile.

Damn, she be looking good in that black Gucci hijab with the white letters. Amina has a beautiful smile, and her dark complexion makes her very sexy. I just might have to snatch her up. She ain't married. I tried to fuck her before, but she on some shit like that I got to start praying and going to Jumuah (Friday prayer at the Masjid) and all that stuff. I told her all that shit could wait. I'm trying to get rich, right now, but damn she make a nigga think twice about it.

I walked to the back to go see Saleem. He had his head down when I walked in the room. "Leem, what's good?"

"As-Salaam-Alaikum," said Saleem.

"Wa-Alaikum-As-Salaam."

"Start greeting Muslims when you see them chump." said Saleem, playfully.

"Yeah, I know. I just be on some other shit at times."

"I know, that's why I'm telling you. Straighten up Ock. What's going on with you though? How the family doing?"

"Mira getting bigger by the day. Eating everything up in the crib."

"Ha, Ha, that's how it is Ock."

"I know!"

"What are you going to name the baby?"

"Abdul Aziz."

"Abdul Aziz?" asked Saleem.

"Yup!"

"That's a beautiful name!"

"Oh, I forgot to tell you. Evon pregnant too."

"Damn, two at the same time, huh?"

"Yeah, she found out that she's having a boy, too."

"What are you going to name him?"

"I was thinking about naming him Tarik."

"Tarik huh. Also a beautiful name. So, we got two young Muslim soldiers coming into the family." said Saleem.

"My Mom is happy as shit. She about to be a young grandmother, but I forgot to tell her about Evon."

"Ah, she'll be alright. I haven't talked to her in a while, I'm going to slide past there today."

"I came past here, though, to put you down about what happened this morning up the way."

"What?"

After giving Unc the run down, he couldn't do nothing, but shake his head. Then he said, "Where Sahih at now?"

"I took him up to his spot in Philly."

"Did anybody see him do it?"

"He said it was only Lil D, his youngbul wit him when he did it."

"You know what? I think it's time to shut that block down. Y'all got to for a minute, because you niggas is drawing up there. Getting all that money and y'all still want to be on the front line, doing crazy shit all the time. And it's stupid shit at that. Now, why would Sahih be gambling with Big Boy for? Big Boy don't have no fucking money. He broke as shit, so that body could have been avoided," said Saleem.

"You right."

"I know I'm right, because you niggas is going to bring the Feds around here and get everybody locked the hell up."

"Why you say that?" I asked.

"Because. Look at it, Rell gets killed on the block number one. After that Young'in and them are out there shooting everything that moves that he think, you hear me, he think is a threat, knowing them niggas don't want no trouble.

For instance, he shot the old head, because he shorted him 300 hundred dollars. Come on Nieem, that's bad for business.

Now this shit with Sahih, I'm going to have to go holla at Big Boy's peoples. I fucks with his brothers and them. They get work from me, so you see what I'm saying. Slow up, because I ain't going to jail for you niggas," Saleem ended, furiously.

"I hear you," was all I could say.

"What's up with that bul Khalil down Delaware, is he straight?"

"What you mean is he straight?" I questioned.

"Is he going to tell under pressure?" Saleem asked, staring me straight in the eyes trying to get a point across to me.

"Naw, he's a soldier Unc."

"I hope so, because it was your idea for him to kill Rell, so he's your problem. That's ya man."

"He straight," I assured.

"What did he do with the gun and all the shit after the murder?" Saleem questioned further.

"I went and took it from him the next day after the murder and threw it in the Delaware River. I burned the clothes with the rental car and everything and I gave him thirty thousand."

"That was a sign right there. When he took the money, he showed that he's easy to be bought. I hope you are sure about this nigga. Was he with you, when you threw the gun away?"

"Naw."

"Okay that's a plus. No gun, no clothes, no evidence. Only his word against yours."

"Saleem I got something else to tell you, too. Do you know a Muslim bul from Philly, named Huss?"

"Yeah, he get money up there in Germantown. Why, what's up with him?"

"Sahih just met this young jawn from up Mount Airy that use to be his girl, or something. He been messing with her for like two weeks now. One night Sahih had her up in his spot all drunk and shit, about to fuck her, then she started talking about the nigga Huss, and how she ain't fucking wit no more hustlers and stuff like that. Anyway, Sahih start asking her a whole bunch of questions about the bul.

She start spilling everything. Where the money at and all that."

"Where he live at? Did she say that, also?"

"Bul live over Jersey in them new town houses they just built."

"I know where you talking about. I was thinking about buying a couple of those and sell them when the prices start going up," said Saleem.

"Anyway Unc, Sahih going to lay on the bul. I told him to get straight on it, so we can grab the bul, before he switch spots."

"You right. What type of girl is she?" Saleem asked.

"Good girl type. Going to college to become a lawyer. Plus, she grew up in Mount Airy and she Ethiopian."

"The Motherland, huh!"

"Yup"

"So, if she is telling Sahih all this shit about her ex-boyfriend, what makes y'all think she won't do the same thing to him?"

"He told her he work construction. Plus, she was drunk as shit, and didn't remember anything about the night before. At least that's what he said."

"I hope he didn't slip up around that girl. Just because she ain't from the streets, she still ain't that green. Let him know that, after y'all get Huss, to move from that spot he at right now, and don't bring her to his next one."

"I'll let him know, but Unc don't worry, I got shit under control up there. We don't have to shut it down, yet." I told him with the straight face.

"You ain't ready for no more work yet?" Saleem probed.

"Naw, I still got a couple of jawns left. That's what was left the last time I checked."

I finished breaking down Saleem on the other little things that was going on, then I left to go holla at my men.

Chapter 10

I pulled up on Boyle Street and saw Shaheed, Young'in and all the youngbuls out there.

Jumping out of the truck, I headed over to the yard they were sitting in. It looked like the niggas was in a deep conversation, because Shaheed was doing all the talking, and everybody else just nodding their heads, every time he said something.

"Sheed... what's going on out here?"

"Ock, I'm just letting these niggas know to be on point, because you know that the nigga Big Boy's peoples might try to do some dumb shit," Shaheed answered.

"Is the police still around there?" I asked him.

"Naw, they been came and took that bitch ass nigga body from around there."

"Oh yeah, Saleem said he going to holla at the bul Big Boy's peoples, too."

"When?"

"I don't know when, but I know he's going to get on top of it, soon as possible. What's the word on who seen the shit happen?"

"Lil D is the only person that exactly seen him do the shit... Word around here is that Sahih did it, but nobody seen him exactly do it," said Shaheed.

"Shaheed, you holla at Lil D yet?"

"Naw, I'm going to pull up on him though and if I even get a whiff that he's going break I'm going to put Young'in on his ass."

"Yeah, I know that's right... You holla at your brother?"

"Naw, I'm going to slide past his spot later on."

"Well, here go his keys and shit. His car parked in front of my spot around the corner. He said to park it in front of your Pop's crib."

"I seen the car around there. I jumped out and knocked on your door, but I figured he jumped in the car wit you... Did y'all get rid   of everything?" Shaheed inquired.

"We took care of all that... Hold up Sheed, let me call Young'in over here with us... Young'in come here man, for second."

Young'in walked over and asked "what's up?"

"What's good wit you?"

"Ah man, you know I'm straight. I was just over there letting them youngbuls know that they will have to stay strapped. They can't be leaving that shit on the ground or on top of the car tires."

While, Young'in was talking a white minivan pulled up and the side door slide open. Boom, Boom, Boom, Boom, Boom, Boom, Boom... Everybody ducked behind the line of cars along Boyle Street. The youngbuls that was in the yard all was laying on the ground, or running to the abandon house to go grab some guns.

When, I heard the van speed off, I yelled, "damn, who the fuck is that?"

"That was Big Boy's brothers right there... Them niggas didn't have no masks on." Shaheed said, "Anybody get hit?"

"Naw, it looks like we cool... Ae that's what I'm telling y'all young niggas to stay strapped for, shit like that," Young'in said to them.

"Them bitch ass niggas didn't want to hit us, because if they did, they would have jumped out of the fucking van...I'm going to kill every last one of them niggas... Ae, Young'in hold this shit down out here. Make sure y'all niggas keep them guns on y'all at all times," I ordered.

"No doubt,"said Young'in.

"Ae Nieem, come on let's jump in my truck and take a ride," said Shaheed.

"Come on Sheed I'm wit that."

We jumped in his truck. That's when Shaheed went on to say "them niggas act like we from Cali or some shit. That corny ass drive by shit... that's some nerd shit. What the fuck ever happen to get your man and that's that?" said Shaheed.

"I don't know Ock. Them niggas is going to pay for that shit though. No bullshit."

"I seen all three of them in that minivan. It looked like a rental minivan, because I never seen nobody in the city driving it... All of them buls in there be up in the Bennett Homes projects. They fuck wit Old head bul, Newme from up there.

I know he didn't give them the green light to do that shit... He got too much respect for us and ya Uncle Saleem... Them niggas did that shit without even thinking or trying to talk or anything. The niggas don't even know what happened," said Shaheed with an angry tone.

"Fuck 'em, that's good they don't want to talk, because I don't want to talk either. So it's all good wit me... Plus on another note, your brother might got a sting for us over in Jersey."

"Who is it?"

"Bul name Huss from up North Philly."

"Oh yeah, I heard of the nigga when I got grabbed by the Feds for that gun case we caught together. Remember, when the State kept your case and the Feds picked mine up? I was locked up with some of his homies. That's all they did was talk about the bul," said Shaheed.

"Well Sahih going to lay on the bul and put us down wit how the nigga move."

"Who put him on Huss?" Shaheed asked.

"Some girl he met up Philly."

"He never told me about her."

"He said he just grabbed her like a month ago."

"Oh, okay then." Shaheed responded.

"Ae Shaheed, won't you drop me off down Delaware man. I got to check up on my baby girl Mira. I haven't talked to her all day. I stayed up the way last night."

"What about your truck?"

"Huh, here go the keys. Give them to Young'in and tell him that he got it for the day... I'm going to chill at home for the rest of the day."

Chapter 11

As soon as I walked in the door, there was my beautiful baby girl heading to the kitchen, in her Victory Secret pajamas. Damn! She look so good. Now, Mira is 5'8 135 pounds. People say she reminds them of Tyra Banks. Mira always wanted to become a model, but I put a stop to all of that, because I didn't want my baby girl walking around half naked and niggas be lusting all over her.

Mira is 17 now and 3 months pregnant. We been together since she was 14. She's the love of my life. Onetime, I damn near paralyzed this nutt ass nigga who tried to holla at her. Mira knows how crazy I am about her. My Mom always tell us that we're made for each other.

I can't wait until she have my youngbul and she can't wait either. That's all Mira's been talking about lately, other than trying to get me out of the streets and move down Georgia by her family, in the boon docks somewhere.

I told her I'd think about it, but for real, all I know is the dope game. I don't want to do shit else, but sell drugs.

"Hey baby, how you doing? Did you win us some money last night?" Mira asked coming out of the kitchen.

I had forgot for a second that I told her that I went down Atlantic City last night. "Naw baby, I lost like 4 stacks. Come here and give me a kiss" I said grabbing her by the waist.

"My friend just called me and said that somebody just did a drive by on ya block. Was you out there? She said you was."

"Yeah, I was out there. I'm cool, though."

"I feel you baby. I'm about to cook some chicken wings and some greens and potatoes to go with it; you hungry?"

"I'm starving" I said kissing Mira on the neck.

"Or do you want me to cook something special for you?"

"Naw, I'm cool wit what you going to make. I'm going to jump in the shower while you cook, okay."

"Don't be long." She said as I took off upstairs.

In the bathroom, I started taking off all my clothes, while looking in the mirror at my 5 ft 7 inch, 150 pound frame. Despite not working out, my six-pack is in there. I guess it comes from playing a lot of sports when I was young.

I went ahead and jumped in the shower and stopped looking in the mirror at myself, like a little conceded bitch or something.

While in the shower I couldn't help but think, damn what am I going to do about Big Boy's fucking brothers and them. If it ain't one thing it's another. I think I'm going to tell Young'in and a couple of other youngbuls to pay them niggas a visit up in that projects of theirs. Them niggas straight violated us today doing that bull shit, and I never be slipping like that. I always keep a gun on me. Suddenly, my thoughts switched to Sahih. I hope he get on top of that tonight. I should call him when I get out of the shower, just to remind him. Naw though, that nigga always on point about some paper. I'm going to let him do his thing.

I wonder how my baby going to react when she finds out that Evon's pregnant. Damn, that's going to break her heart.

I be swearing up and down that I don't be fucking around on her and she be believing me too. Mira never heard about me with any other broads, I make sure I let them know from the rip that I got a girl. As a matter of fact, I tell them I got a wife at home and that if we going to be fucking, then they got to respect that. Suddenly, the bathroom door opened up, "Umm, look at my baby." Mira said as she slipped off her pajamas.

She had no panties or anything else underneath. My dick got hard as shit. So I asked, "What, you getting in with me?"

"Yup."

When she got in the shower, I started kissing her pecan titties with nice and round nipples poking out; licking all around them.

"Umm Nieem, that feels good."

I started kissing on them nice beautiful lips of hers, while grabbing her nice petite waist. Mira, grinding her pussy against my dick. And started to moan all crazy, that's when I went down, kissing her stomach and rubbing it. From there I traveled straight down to licking her pussy. She grabbed my head, pushing it back and forth while I tongue fucked her. "Umm, Nieem that feels so good... Oh baby keep licking that spot right there. Oh baby I'm about to... Oh baby." Mira said, while leaning back on the shower wall. Now, I turned her around and slide my dick in her wet pussy from the back, giving her nice and long strokes.

She start fucking me back, with one hand on the wall. With her free hand, she reached around and grabbed my leg. "Fuck me harder baby," Mira begged.

I started giving her nice, short and hard strokes, and I could feel my dick getting bigger by the stroke. "Oh baby, this pussy feel so good, and so wet." When Mira heard me say that, she turned over and grabbed my dick and start sucking the shit out of it, with deep long strokes. She only got 5 in, before I started cumming like crazy. Mira kept sucking making sure everything was out. "Damn, I love you girl!" I told her.

"I'm going to let you finish taking your shower, now. I just had to come in get me some, since last night you didn't come home... I'm going to finish cooking. I'll get in the shower when you're done."

"For round two, huh?"

"I hope so!" She said with a seductive look, before leaving out.

Chapter 12

I'm glad I stayed in all day yesterday, because I got to spend some time with my baby. These past couple of months been hectic and I been ripping and running.

I haven't even told my Mom that Evon is pregnant I'm surprised her Mom didn't call mine already. They both work together and been good friends for many years.

I pulled out the S550 today to go make a couple of runs. I got to go check out Khalil and R down here while I'm in Delaware, and pick this paper up that they got waiting on me. As I'm thinking this to myself the phone rang.

"Yo, what's up?"

"What's good wit you Old head?" Young'in voice barked.

"I'm just coming out. How everything look up there?"

"It's all good out there. Me and Shaheed went to see Sahih last night. I drove his car up Philly to his spot. Then we went and got something to eat up in Dave and Buster's on Delaware Ave." said Young'in.

"He put y'all on the new babe he met up there?"

"Yeah, but I'll holla at you later on that."

"I feel you. You got my truck?"

"Yeah, I was about to slide pass the carwash and get it cleaned," said Young'in.

"Which one?"

"The one on 9th street; down the street from the High (Chester High School)."

"Young'in be careful. You know them wild cowboys probably still running around stressing about they brother."

"I know, but fuck them chumps. I ain't hiding from them lame ass niggas. They hip to me." Young'in said, cockily.

"Ae Young'in, you ain't the only nigga that will push a nigga shit back, or the only one with a gun. So be smart and use ya head, instead of going off your pride and emotions and shit."

"I feel you Ock. I'm just going up the way to see what them youngbuls up there doing."

"I'll be down there in a minute. I got to holla at my peoples on 2-4 for a minute... Matter of fact, I'm on the block right now about to pull up on him... I'm going to get wit you, Young'in."

"Aight," He said then hung up.

I rolled down the window and told Khalil, let me pull over.

Jumping out of my black on black S550 Benz I couldn't help but notice all the niggas looking at that bitch, seeing how clean it was. I didn't have any rims on it, just the regular ones dipped in chrome. As a matter of fact, I think I'm the only hustling nigga in Chester and Delaware that got this car. I know a couple of Philly buls wit them, but I haven't seen one down here yet.

"Khalil, what's up wit you Ock?"

"Ah man, I'm chilling. I see you brought that bitch catcher out today... You make a nigga want to go and grab the all white jawn on your ass," said Khalil.

"How everything going on down here. You need any more work, because I'm about to make a move, so let me know what's good."

"I need some more. These junkies loving that last issue. They thought I went to Columbia myself and grabbed that shit..." Khalil said with a smile.

"Ha, Ha... My other peoples saying the same thing. I hope the next jawn I grab be the same way. I'm getting it from the same person. You got the rest of that money?"

"Yeah, plus I'm giving you half of the money for the next pack now. And, when you bring it, I'll have the other half. Walk me around here to my little spot that I just rented to chill in when I'm around here." said Khalil.

As we are walking I see the undercover cops riding around, just staring and taking pictures of the buls on the corner we passed, which was 22nd street. "Yo, who the fuck is that, the Feds?"

"Yeah, the nigga N.Y. around here just robbed the Feds for a hundred thousand. They locked him up last week with a gun. And they told him that if he work for them, they would let him back out, and he agreed to do it. They put a wire on the nigga and gave him a hundred thousand to line up the bul Khalif from down Riverside, but the bul pulled a fast one on them. He tore the wire off and left it in the spot and took the first train back to New York. They think he still around here somewhere though, but the nigga long gone." Khalil said, all in the same breath.

"You think they watching your block too?"

"Naw, because I didn't even speak to the grimy ass nigga... I was going to blow his head off a couple of weeks ago." Khalil said with anger in his tone.

"For what? What the bul do?"

"We was all up in Ambrosas one night, and when I say all of us, I mean my squad was in there, and all them 22st street niggas was too; even though we all fuck wit each other I don't fuck wit him. Anyway though, the nigga NY was all drunk and shit and started talking about how he was going to start putting his work all over the North Side of Delaware, on some either get down or lay down shit.

My man pulled my coat to what the nigga was saying, so I stepped to him. I knew I should've just laid on the nigga when we got back around the way, but the liquor had my head fucked up and was doing the talking and thinking for me. Anyway though, I stepped to him and asked, what the fuck is all this shit you talking about taking over the North Side... He started bitching up and shit, talking 'bout, naw it ain't like that. I fuck wit y'all niggas and I know you niggas ain't going for no shit like that and why would he try us and all that bull shit.

After that, I pulled my man Yusef (Sef) to the side and told him that he needed to check this nigga, or I'm going to, because the nigga just gave us all a silent threat and the nigga from New York, not from Delaware. And that I didn't have no problem killing this clown, because I hate New York niggas anyway because them faggots robbed me for 25 thousand when I was a youngbul coming up... You remember that, don't you?" Khalil asked.

"I remember that shit. Nine thousand of it, you was holding for me."

"Anyway, the Feds really saved his ass, because after he got locked up with that gun Sef gave me the green light to rock the nigga because they thought he was going snitch being that he was a three time felon," said Khalil.

By the time he finished telling me everything, we was finally at his house. We go in and I saw the money green Italian leather sofa set, with an all glass dining room set. He didn't have any T.V. in the living room; only a little Bose radio system in the corner.

"Nie have a seat, while I go upstairs and grab the money."

I thought to myself, boy he lucky that he my man and he put that work in for me, without asking questions, because I would definitely have sent Young'in in this joint.

"Here you go, it's a hundred and fifty thousand. I want my usual." said Khalil, throwing a bag in my lap.

"What you doing tonight?" I asked him.

"I'm thinking about getting wit this little college girl I met down Delaware State (Del-State). She want to spend some time with me, before she go back to school this semester," he answered.

"Aight. Come on, walk me back around the corner to my car."

"Come on Ock," said Khalil.

After me and Khalil gave each other dap I pulled off and put all the money in the trunk. My next stop was to see my man R. I rode past his people's spot at the bottom of 2-4 by the park, and didn't see his car out there, so I kept it moving. I'll catch up wit him later on or something, I thought.

◆　　◆　　◆

After cruising around Delaware, I finally made it back to the city. Pulling into the Gardens, everything was looking good; kids out playing like any usual summer day. Shaheed, Young'in and the rest of the crew was off to the side, out there grinding.

Young'in was directing traffic, while the youngbuls went hand to hand.

"Shaheed, what you doing for them today?"

"Ah man, I can't call it, just another day big fella," Shaheed answered.

"I hear that. What's up wit Sahih? You tell him about them niggas coming through yesterday with that bull shit?"

"I put him down. He also told me that, if we wanted to, we could grab Huss tonight. We ready. Is you wit it?" Shaheed asked.

"No doubt, let's go get this paper, and while we're taking care of that, I think Young'in and them should go pay Big Boy's brothers a fuckin' visit. What you think?"

"Damn right. Ae Nieem, one thing for sure and two things for certain, these niggas know that them Young Gunz from up on Boyle Street ain't going for none of that shit," Shaheed stated matter-of-factly.

"Young'in, come here for a second."

He walked over to us and I told him, "Look, we need you and a couple of youngbuls to go pay them niggas up the Bennett a visit."

"We need you to go up there and make an example, Young Gunz style," Shaheed chipped in.

"I'm on top of it. I found out earlier where them buls be chilling at up in the projects... They got this young jawn named Keyana. They be using her house to hold the work. Her spot is right by the alleyway. It would be easy for us to walk through the alley and lay on them buls." Young'in said, amped up.

"Then make it happen, tonight. We ain't going to be around, so watch over the whole thing, aight!" I told him.

"Yeah, I got y'all."

"No fuck up's Young'in. This shit is serious," I added with much emphasis.

Chapter 13

Darkness had finally set in, while me, Shaheed and Sahih was sitting in the car, about to go and pull this sting off in Jersey.

"Aight look homz, we going to park the car around back.

We're going to break in the house, because when he got the crib he didn't put no alarm in. We are going to search the house first and if we don't find nothing, then we'll wait and make him take us to the money... This should be easy," said Sahih.

"What if there is a alarm in the spot, then we fuck the whole thing up," said Shaheed,

"Look homz, I told y'all I did homework on this shit, so don't second guess me." Sahih said playfully, but was serious.

"Yeah, you right. Come on let's do this!" I told Sahih.

◆　◆　◆

Meanwhile back in Chester, Young'in and his right hand man C, was laying and waiting in the alleyway up in the Bennett Homes Projects. Now, C is another crazy ass youngbul. Him and Young'in around the same age. They been the best of friends for years. C is a high yellow, slim, but toned youngbul. He lives around on Park Terrace, down the street from my spot.

C just came home from beating a double homicide in the State. Now he back at it again fucking with Young'in. As a matter of fact, Young'in was the reason that he caught that double homicide, to begin with.

One night they were coming from a club up Philly with these girls they met in the club. They took them to Young'in spot up in the Gardens. Little did they know that the nigga Kasul from over the Eastside had put these two bitches on C and Young'in, because they had robbed Kasul youngbul in a stash house for twenty stacks. So as they're in the house, C got one of the girls in the room with him and Young'in in the other room with the other girl. The girl start sucking C dick, and before he was about to start fucking her she told him to hold up, that she had to use the bathroom real bad. She went downstairs to unlock the door to let the two niggas in the house.

C was suspicious because she was taking too long to use the bathroom, so he got up and walked in the hallway and looked down the steps and seen the two buls coming in the spot. He rushed in the room and grabbed his gun, then ran to the room door to use as a shield, and started shooting. He hit both of them twice, but he fired 15 shots from his 9mm.

The girl was screaming like shit, while C ran downstairs past the two dead niggas, and grabbed the bitch that opened the door.

Young'in came out of the room with gun in hand, asking C what happened. He yelled to Young'in that the bitches tried to get them killed.

Young'in immediately turned the gun on the bitch he had. C told Young'in to hurry up and tie the girls up and take them out the back of the house and kill them, while he stay there and take the rap for shooting the two buls.

The Cops locked C up with the weapon and everything. He went to trial and beat the case on self-defense, because the two buls had masks on with silencers on the guns. A week later, the girls were found dead in an abandoned house with two head shots a piece.

C sat for a whole year on the double homicide. If it wasn't for Young'in wanting to take them two girls to the house with them that night, he would've never caught them two bodies. Now C is back at it again not even home a month. Here he is, laying in an alleyway up the Bennett Home projects, about to kill again.

Young'in tip toed to the window. One of the blinds was slightly broken, so he could see all three of Big Boy's brothers at the table, counting money. There were two girls in there, also. One sat on one of the brother's lap, and the other was on the couch, watching T.V.

Young'in waved C over. They both were dressed in all black army fatigues, with bullet proof vests on, just in case the niggas start shooting back. He whispers in C ear, giving him the run-down of how many people were inside and all of their positions.

Also Young'in told him that he's going to kick the door in and they were going in firing.

"1, 2, 3," It took Young'in two kicks, instead of one. That gave the brothers a split second to react.

C ran in blazing from the gate with his A.K., saying this is from the Young Gunz mutha fuckas. One of the brothers jumped up from the table and started shooting, but he didn't hit anybody. C cut him down with the A.K.

Young'in came in behind him finishing off the other two. The girl that was sitting on one of the brother's lap jumped up off the ground and tried to run out the door. Young'in gave her all head shoots. The girl was dead, before she even touched the ground. Now the other girl that was watching T.V. was just stuck there sitting on the couch screaming. Young'in told C to deal with her, while he grab the money. He put all the money on the table into a duffle bag that was laying on the ground, next to the dead body.

C, on the other hand shot the screaming bitch twice in the chest, and said to his self in a low voice, "no witnesses bitch."

They ran out the back door into the dark of the alleyway, hearing the sounds of police sirens in the air.

◆　　◆　　◆

Meanwhile back in Jersey, me, Shaheed, and Sahih broke the backdoor's glass window and let ourselves into the house, with guns in our hand. All the lights were off, except in the kitchen. I walked in the living room and turned the light on. The place was decorated with a money green leather sofa set, hard wood floors and all types of expensive paintings on the wall, including big ass chandeliers hanging from the ceiling.

I went upstairs to check the rooms. Shaheed's job was to go down in the basement and check for anything down there. Sahih was to check the living room for any wall safes. After we all went our ways Sahih turned the lights back off, just in case Huss pulled up to the spot.

We were all connected by walkie-talkie, to notify each other in case of any surprises while we were separated throughout the house.

Sahih said the girl told him that in his walk in closet he had a safe. So, to see if she was telling the truth, or was just drunk. I went into the master bedroom, where it was laid out with a big 50 inch T.V., king size bed, with his and her bathrooms. I ran over to the dresser and started grabbing all these Rolex's and platinum chains.

Then I put my attention on the walk in closets. I went in the one with the most clothes. I reached for my pocket knife that I always keep when I go on a sting, just in case I have to cut a telephone line before we run up in the house. I got on my knees and started feeling around on the floor, trying to find the safe. Bingo! I found it under a box of shoes, but he got the carpet covering it. It looks like he used a staple gun to put the carpet back down, so you can't notice it's been moved.

I cut the carpet. Pulling it back I saw a big safe in the floor. "I found the safe in the closet, but ain't no way we're going to be able to take this out the house," I said, alerting Sahih and Shaheed through the walkie.

"I found a safe behind the picture down here too and I'm thinking the same thing," Sahih responded.

"So I guess we're going to have to stay and wait on the nigga. Come on down in the living room." Shaheed's voice came through.

We all met up in the living room.

"Look me and Nieem are going to stay in the house Sahih. You go and move the car, and let us know when he pulls up. If he don't come by 2:00 in the morning, then we'll shoot the damn safes open. Nobody should hear because the houses are not connected to nobody else's." Shaheed said.

"Aight I'm gone then, but just make it clean and quick when he comes. Plus, I'm going to cut the phone line when I leave." Sahih answered.

No sooner than we're saying all this, we see car lights pulling up in front of the house. We all ducked until the lights went off. I get up slow and looked out the window and saw a nigga and a broad walking up, laughing and smiling. They got out of an all white Range. I told them that might be him walking to the house, now, and that he got some light skin girl with him.

We all crawled to the kitchen. I was thinking to myself, I'm glad Sahih turned the lights out, because I was drawing turning them on.

When we got to the kitchen we all stood up. Shaheed was in front. Sahih was second and I was third, because I was the smallest out of them.

We heard them open the front door, then close it behind them. The two of them start walking towards the kitchen.

As soon as Shaheed seen him walk into the light. He smacked Huss across the face with the big ass Desert Eagle.

Sahih ran around Huss and grabbed the girl by the hair. She started screaming, "please don't kill me."

Sahih said "shut up you dumb ass bitch, or else I'll shut you up."

While, Shaheed got the gun on him I went and took the cord off the phone, plus grabbed some of his expensive bed sheets and tied him up with them.

Sahih had the girl by her hair, with a gun in her face. I passed him some telephone cord to tie her up also.

"Huss you know what it is nigga. We came to get this paper. Now, if you want to live, just give us the money and we're gone, or else we'll leave you here stinking," said Shaheed.

"I'm not giving you nigga's shit... Y'all going to kill me anyway."Huss said aggressively.

I told Huss "you think we playing pussy... Let me show you we mean business...Sahih give me that bitch." Boom, Boom. "Nigga we ain't playing." I shot the girl twice in the head.

"Man, fuck that bitch. She a whore anyway." Huss barked.

"Nieem pull his pants down, while I go grab a knife." said Sahih, who went and grabbed a butcher knife. "Pull that nigga boxers down. We're going to see how tough the bul really is. I'm going to cut the left nutt first."

"Wait, wait, wait. I got some money in that safe behind the picture over there." He said nervously.

I asked him, "What's the number pussy?"

"9-11-35-01-22" Huss responded quickly.

I go and open the safe and get five stacks of money. "Nigga, you think this shit a game?" Boom! I shoot him in the knee cap.

"Ah shit, I got more in another safe upstairs. That's the rest of it, I swear," Huss cried.

"What's the number? Bitch ass nigga and it better be some more change in there." I told him before going to check it.

"9-462-843-494" He said in a whimpering voice.

I go upstairs to get the rest of the money out of the safe.

Sahih took the money to the car and came back with some gasoline in a container. "We got to burn the place. My glove came off in here, and I don't know what my finger prints might be on."

He started pouring gasoline all thru the house. When Sahih was ready, Shaheed popped Huss twice in the chest. Sahih lit the fire and we were on our way back to the city of Chester.

Chapter 14

The next day, after the sting I went and met with Uncle Saleem, to put him down on everything that's been going on in the past couple of days.

I found Saleem sitting in the back of Ameer's, reading a newspaper.

Soon as he saw me, he shook his head saying "y'all drawing out there. It's all over the city that y'all did that up the Bennett. Nieem, that's bad for business. Nobody is going to want to deal with no wild cowboys." Saleem said pointedly.

"Unc they did a driveby up the way in broad daylight. What was I supposed to do? I wasn't going to move on them because I thought you was going to get wit their Old head and try to bring some sort of peace to the whole thing, but then they pulled that bull crap. We wanted to make an example to everybody that them buls the Young Gunz from Killa Hill ain't bull shitting. Either you are going to respect them or you're going to fear them." I said raising my voice a little.

"So who did it? They say two people ran from the scene."

"Young'in and C did it."

"I hope all these youngbuls you been sending out to kill all these people stand tall when them Feds start knocking on the doors." Saleem said incredulously.

"They are fucking soldiers Unc. I know for sure they'll stand tall."

"Don't ever say you know anything for sure. When them people start throwing life sentences around, and start talking about giving that needle out, the best of them roll over. Believe me; I've seen it happen over and over again. And remember, nothing in life is for sure except death."

"Yeah, I feel you Unc. Plus, we went out to Jersey last night and grabbed that bul Huss. We took only 250,000 from him. We had to kill him and a broad that was with him because we forgot to wear masks and Sahih lost his glove in there while we was searching the house. We burned the house down, though."

"Nieem, Nieem, why so much killing?"

"I know Saleem, I told myself that I'm going to fall back for a little and play the cut. It seems like I stay in the mix of shit, but Unc you know that killing comes in the line of work we do. It's either kill or be killed and I would rather be judged by 12 instead of carried by 6... You feel me?"

"Yeah, I feel you, but one thing for sure and two things for certain. You better start covering your tracks, because too many people are involved in these murders. I'm just giving you some food for thought. So how the block doing?" Saleem questioned.

"I came to grab some work from you. What you got for me?"

"I'm waiting on it as we speak, so get wit me early tomorrow." Unc replied.

"Plus I got a little something for you, from the sting we just got... It's nothing major, just a little 20 thousand for you to play around wit or something. I'll bring it by tomorrow, when I come for that work."

"Yeah, I would like that. I'm going over to offer Hajj (a pilgrimage Muslims make once a year) in Mecca this year. It comes in around December. I could use that to pay for the trip. What's up wit Sahih and Shaheed?"

"Sahih still laying low, it's only been a couple of days since that shit happened. No cops ain't been around but he still going to wait it out for a minute. Shaheed good though, I haven't talked to him today. Well, I'm about to go make a run real quick. I'm going to get wit you tomorrow. As-Salaam-Alaikum."

"Wa-Alaikum-As-Salaam." said Saleem.

◆　　◆　　◆

Back around the neighborhood, police was everywhere. I pulled my S550 over. Jumping out of the car, I headed over to my man Roe, "Roe, what's up wit you?"

"Ae Nieem, I'm mad as shit. This fucking junkie bitch pulled off wit one of my youngbuls pack, and when she got to the corner of the block, the bul Tiz threw a brick at her window and it hit her in the face. The car went out of control and ran the youngbul lil Brad over," Roe said in a hurtful tone.

"Damn, youngbul was only like 10 or 11... Hun?"

"He was 10. When she hit lil Brad, her truck was stuck on top of him. Everybody ran up there and tried to lift the truck up. Nieem that shit was crazy, fire was coming from the engine and shit. It looked like a scene from a movie or something. By the time we grabbed him from under the truck, he was dead already. When somebody yelled he was gone, Hass ran up on the car and shot that bitch once in the head and twice in the chest. Everybody around this bitch is pissed. They got detectives everywhere, trying to question people, but so far ain't nobody talking." Roe finished.

"Damn that's fucked up about youngbul. I use to fuck wit his little ass. He used to always ask me for a job. I use to tell him, when you get a little older young'in."

"Nieem, I'm about to go walk around to the store. I hate being around all these damn police." said Roe.

"Yeah, I feel you. I'm going to get wit you later. I'm about to walk down to Boyle Street, to see if Young'in and them out there." As I'm walking past the crime scene, I'm just thinking to myself; damn this has been a long and dangerous summer.

I walked down like a block from Boyle St. and I see Evon and her girls leaning on the gate just watching the police up the street investigating the whole crime scene. She saw me, and ran across the street hugging me and crying, telling me how much she loves me and don't want nothing to happen to me.

I gave her a kiss and wiped her tears, and let her know that everything is going to be alright, and to please stop worrying and stressing for the baby's sake.

"I know baby, you're right. I just hate to see anything happen to you. I need you to be here for me and the baby. It just been too much violent shit going on around here." said Evon.

"Baby calm down, everything is going to be aight. I'm going to be here for you and my youngbul; come on let's walk around my spot. I missed you. I haven't been spending enough time wit you."

Me and Evon walked around to my spot. I still haven't given her a key yet. I think I am though, because it's about time that I really start taking care of my girl. She's about to have my baby. Plus, I'm really in love with her.

We get to the door of my apartment, and it was slightly open. I kicked the door open, and ran straight in there, checking all of the rooms. The house was empty.

"What's wrong wit you boy? Running in there with no gun on you?" Evon said, catching my attention.

"I was slipping, huh?"

"Yup."

I started looking around. "Damn, look at the window. It's broke. That's probably where they came in at. Let me check the closet for my safe? Damn it's gone. I had 2 bricks and 300,000 thousand in there. Damn I was been supposed to get that shit out of here. I'm going to kill them mutha fuck'as who did this."

"But, you don't know who did it." said Evon.

"I'm going to find out though." I walked in the living room and sat down on the couch, fucked up in the head, 'How in the hell I get caught slipping like that?' I thought.

Evon started cleaning up the mess that they made looking around for whatever they could find. When Evon was done, she came over to the couch and tried to cheer me up. "Baby it's going to be alright. You can make the money back." She said

"Evon, that's a lot of damn money that I have to make back," I snapped. "Plus, I was just about to give you a key, so that you can stay here with me. You probably don't want to stay in here now, hun?"

"Hell no. They could have broke in, while I was in here sleeping and took some pussy, or something. As a matter of fact, let's get out of here. Where your car at?"

"I left it up on the block earlier. We cool though; I got a gun in here that they didn't take. I keep it in my jacket, so we're cool."

I walked Evon home, then grabbed my car and rode down Boyle Street; I saw Young'in and C out there, so I jumped out to holla at them niggas.

"Nieem, what's good wit you Ock?" Young'in asked then we shook hands.

"Young'in a nigga ran in my spot around the corner. It had to be late last night after I dropped some money off there. I just jammed a nigga, and a nigga get me the same night. That shit crazy huh!" I almost laughed.

"Damn Ock, who the fuck disrespected my man like that? What did they take?" Young'in inquired.

"My mutha fuckin' safe."

"C come here right quick." Young'in called.

"What's up?" C asked, walking over.

"Ae, C you see any niggas around by your crib last night, looking suspicions or carrying a safe or something? Mutha fuck'a ran up in my spot."

"Matter of fact, I did see some buls parked in front of my house, just staring up there in the direction of ya spot. I paid no attention to it, though, because you know that them bitches that strip stay across from you. I thought they was waiting for one of them, or something like that. But the bul looked like Jay that be up 8th street with R and them." C pointed out.

"Yeah, I fuck wit the bul R, too. Let me call him and see what type time his man on. Hold up for a second fellas." I called R, and he picked up on the second ring, "R, what's good wit you?"

"I'm chilling Ock. What you been up to? I heard what happened to the youngbul lil Brad. That shit was fucked up."

"You hear about what happened last night, too?"

"Naw, what?" He asked in a concerned way.

"I got word that ya man Jay ran up in my spot. Him and another bul."

"Yeah?" R replied, sounding genuinely surprised.

"Yeah. Let bul know Ock that I need all my shit back. And, only on the strength that I fuck wit you, I'm not going to kill him for that shit." I came back with.

"Me and you go way back. Let me holla at the bul. He told me that he got a nigga last night, but he didn't say it was you... He told me it was another bul, shit."

"Who shit he say it was?"

"That bitch ass nigga from the Lamokin Village (L.V.) named Money Green. The babe Safiyah from up there told him that it was Money Green's spot." said R.

"I know that bitch."

"But, dig this homz. Let me make a phone call and I'm going to get that back for you on the strength that you my man."

"No doubt. I would do the same for you."

"I'll call you back in a minute." R said, then disconnected.

I walked back over to Young'in and C. And told them "the bul R said he gonna get my shit back. Guess who put the bul on me?"

"Who?" Young'in and C said at the same time.

"The babe Safiyah from around the Cutt Off. She be with my girl Evon."

"How she know where your safe was at?" asked C.

"Because that use to be my young jawn before, until I caught her fucking wit this nigga from down Delaware that be wit my man Khalil... He had the little bitch on tape eating his dick all up, fuckin' her in the ass and everything. When I found this out, I beat the shit out of her, took all her clothes, and that Lexus coupe I brought for her birthday. She had a key to the spot around the crib, but I never told her about no money being in there. I guess she must've been searching the house when I wasn't there. I haven't fucked wit her in a whole year.

My girl Evon said she be saying little fly shit out her mouth about me. But when Evon check her, she be like damn I was only playing. Why you trying to fight me over a nigga?"

"So how we going to deal wit the bitch Nieem? If you want me to, I'll cut that bitch throat for you." C offered.

"Naw, I don't want to kill her. I want that nasty bitch to suffer. I just need one of y'all to take a metal bat and give her two good swings to the back of the fuckin' head. Put that bitch in a wheel chair for the rest of her life."

"Shit, we can do that tonight when them bitches be all drunk after the bar closes. I just hope she goes home tonight. Plus, we took care of them buls last night. We had to kill the two girls too, because you know how we roll, no face, no case, so they had to go. We caught them buls counting money. It was only 25,000 thousand, nothing major. You want a break down out of that?" Young'in asked.

"Naw, y'all put the work in, y'all keep the change. What the block did today?"

"We only made 4,500 hundred today because of what happened to the youngbul lil Brad, so I just shut shop down. We still got a half of jawn left, though. Plus the police gripped Hass up too for killing the junkie bitch that hit lil Brad. Shit was crazy out here Ock. Mutha fucka's was about to riot out this bitch, when they grabbed Hass. The Feds and everything was out here with big ass AR 15's, ready to kill them a nigga. I was just looking, playing the cutt, saying to myself, how the fuck they let them grab him that easy? I would have went out in the blaze of glory, homz." Young'in replied.

"Because, ya ass shot the fuck out." I told him, playfully.

"Yeah, you might be right, but dig this Ock; I made a promise to myself when I was doing my last bid. I'm never going to let these crackers put me in the trick bag again.

Them cells is cold and lonely at night. That shit is for nutt ass niggas, not niggas like us, that's about that fuckin' paper, you feel me, homz?" Young'in said with a serious expression.

"I feel you homz, I'm going out the same way, in a blaze of glory. Fuck'em, I'll see 'em in hell," C chipped in.

"I see why you two crazy niggas be together, now. Hold up, let me answer my horn." I told them. "R, what's up?"

"Nieem I got everything back for you. Where you at, so I can bring it to you?"

"I'm sitting on Boyle St. right now, but I want you to meet me at the Mobil gas station on 9th Street, instead of up here. I'm going to be in my S550. How long is it going to take you to get there?" I questioned.

"10 minutes... I'm riding down 9th Street now. I'm up in my 500 today." said R.

"Aight" We both hung up the phone. I walked back over to Young'in and C.

"What happen homz?" Young'in asked.

"I'm about to go meet him right now. Come take this ride wit me y'all." We all jumped in my car and rode down to the gas station, which was only down the street and around the corner from the Gardens. When I pulled in the gas station, I see R's all green 500 Benz parked by the gas pump. His car got tints on it, so I really couldn't see inside being that it was dark outside, but when I rode in front of the car I saw him and the bul Jay inside. I told my youngbuls to chill, because they wanted to get at the bul Jay for disrespecting me.

I pulled over on the other side of the gas pump. As I'm parking Jay jumped out of the car, then we all exited.

"As-Salaam-Alaikum, Ock." R greeted.

"Wa-Alaikum-As-Salaam," I told him back.

"Nieem I brought Jay with me just, so you'll know that he was not intending to rob you on purpose. While y'all rapping, I'm going to grab the money for you." said R.

"Ae, Young'in grab that money from him." I told him.

"Nieem, the bitch played me and I'm going to get at her about that... I really thought that was the bul Money Green spot. I didn't think you would be living up there... My bad, though." Jay said, apologetically.

"Don't worry about it. Plus, I'm going to take care of that bitch. Everything cool homz, I got my money back, that's all I wanted." I told him. After, Young'in put the money in the trunk of my car, we both gave our departing words, then R told me to get wit him tomorrow.

We finally made it back up the Gardens, after I dropped the money off back at the apartment. I stayed with Young'in and C most of the night, just laughing, joking, and smoking a lot of weed. We were staying out late tonight so we could wait on the chick Safiyah to leave the bar.

I rode down Reflections on 9th Street. This is the bar that mostly everybody on the Westside of Chester go to. It was no later than 1:55am and the bar was about to close. I sent C in there to buy a case of Heinekens, and to see if she was in there. He came back out and told us that she's in there with Shelly from around the Cutt Off. I put a plan together as we pulled off. "Ae Young'in , these bitches is walking back up the way, so what I want you and C to do is, wait in the alleyway by the school, because they're going to walk past there.

Grab the masks and the metal bat I got in the trunk," I told them. After they grab the stuff I finished telling them the plan. "Now Young'in , I want you to be the one to punish her. C you just pull the gun out and scare Shelly. Did they see you in the bar?" I asked him.

"Naw, they didn't pay no attention to me, because they was drunk as shit." C replied surely.

"Aight dig this homz. This is the alleyway that y'all are going to wait in. The bar is only around the corner. I'm going to be waiting on the next block." I told them.

"We good from here, Ock" said Young'in .

I pulled off, heading around the corner. I found a parking space on the dark side of the street. No less than five minutes later, I saw them running to the car laughing.

"I was smacking that bitch in the back hard as shit. All I kept hearing was crack, crack, crack. I think I broke her back because when I was done she was just moaning not moving at all." Young'in joked.

"I put the babe Shelly face down on the ground; I didn't hurt her, though. She was just crying the whole time." C interrupted.

"Fuck the babe Safiyah. That's what you get when you want to play the game. It's either kill or be killed. The bitch lucky, she wasn't killed for that stunt," I told them.

Chapter 15

Six months later in February of 2000

Everything was going well. The block is pulling in 10,000 a day, my baby Mira had my first boy named Abdul Aziz, and Evon had my other boy Tarik. They were twelve days apart. I even moved her into her own crib.

Mira almost left me over the fact that I had another wife and another baby. I had to shower her with some gifts and promises to be faithful, and then I asked her to marry me. She was happy as shit.

My man Sahih came back out and everything was back to normal.

There were no problems from none of those fuckin' suckers running around here in the city.

My Uncle Saleem was happy that I started falling back, and staying out of dumb shit. He even went and offered Hajj this year, him and one of his wives. So he was real excited about that. Unc kept trying to convince me to go next year, but how can I go; I'm not even praying now. Plus, I'm too much in the dunya all crazy.

The babe Safiyah was alright after all, minus some broken ribs. She knew that Young'in and C did it and threatened to tell on them, until I paid her some hush money. After all, I used to love this broad. Plus, I didn't need that unwanted attention, because everybody knew that I got her beat up.

It was a cold winter day when I came from out my house, down in Delaware. I had sold my S550 and went and grabbed an all black on black Yukon. After getting off of the phone with my man Shaheed, I was going to meet him in Chester because something important had came up, but he changed his mind and told me to meet him at Sahih's house up Philly, and that everybody was up there waiting on me.

I drove up Philly to holla at my man and them. I parked my truck and got out and knocked on the door.

"Come on in playa, what's good Ock?" said Sahih.

"Ah man, I can't complain... What's going on with y'all fellas?"

"What's up Ock?" said Shaheed.

After, we made a little bit of small talk, we got down to business.

It was me, Shaheed, Sahih and Young'in at the spot. When I came in Young'in was in the bathroom, the whole time, taking a shit. When he was done me and him greeted each other and then he said "ae fellas, I got everybody together because me and C just got plugged in with these two Cops... Before anybody talk let me explain everything. My man C be fuckin' this young jawn in Aston. Her dad is a Chester Police Detective. The cop pushed up on C talking about he trying to holla at one of y'all three. C told the nigga that, that was straight out of the question. He told him that none of y'all would ever do business with a cop. So he told C that the type of information I got, they would give anything to get it. So, C told him to break it down for him, and he would relay the message to who it was suppose to be given to. The cop went on and told C that him and a narcotic officer would like to help us out. They said they see we're getting a lot of money now, and they could help us get even more by them being our eyes and ears around town and in the station. He said they was trying to do all this for a small fee of 2,000 thousand a month for each of them."

"So, where is C right now?" I asked.

"We waiting for him to pull up," said Young'in.

"Matter of fact, that's him knocking on the door now," said Sahih.

C came in and greeted everybody and started talking straight business.

"I told them up to the point when they gave the price and you can fill them in on all the rest," said Young'in.

"Yeah, the babe Chasity I fuck wit, dad is a Homicide Detective with the Chester Police. Well him and his friend, which is a narcotic cop, is trying get on the team. I told them that if we deal with them, everything will have to go thru me, because none of y'all are going to deal wit them. I told them that I would run it pass y'all and give him an answer by this week," C ended.

"What is this information that he's got that mutha fuck'as would kill for?" asked Shaheed.

"I was going to get to that at the end, but he told me that the youngbul Don is telling on Sahih about how he works for him and about the murder of Rell." C answered.

"That Cop fuckin' lying C... Did he show you paper work?" Sahih questioned.

"He showed me paper work of him breaking down how you and Shaheed run that heroin on the block, and how Nieem got Young'in running the weed and powder sales up there, too. So yeah, I seen it wit my own eyes and he also said that the Feds been trying to get him to wear a wire and all that and that they was trying to build a RICO case against us. That shit they be booking the Mafia wit," said C.

"We know what the fuck it is. Did you see paper work on the murder of Rell?" Sahih asked.

"Naw, so, what y'all think about dude?" C said staring at us all.

"I think he a good asset for us, but can we trust him when we kill this Federal witness?" I asked.

"That's my whole concern." Sahih followed.

"Mine too!" came Shaheed.

"I say we say fuck it, and kill all loose ends tying us to any murders. Rock the youngbul and the fuckin' Cops, because he is going to be a fuckin' witness against us when he get his ass in a sling." said Young'in.

"You can't just go around killing Cops Ock. Drug dealers and other hood niggas is cool. Not no cops, though. Let me holla at my peoples first, before we make any decisions," I told them.

"In the mean time, Young'in and C, y'all keep an eye on lil Don," Sahih ordered.

Chapter 16

After the meeting with my squad, I went straight to holla at my Uncle Saleem and put him down on what's happening.

I entered into the restaurant and saw him behind the cash register, taking a customer's money.

"As-Salaam-Alaikum, Saleem."

"Wa-Alaikum-As-Salaam," he answered in a seemingly good mood.

"I got something important to holla at you about," I said moving around the counter,

"Come on, let's go to the back."

"Saleem, we got a big problem... The youngbul C from up the way got this young jawn that he be fuckin' named Chasity, right, and her dad is a Chester Police Detective in the Homicide Unit, the cop wants us to pay him to be our source inside the police station. You know like keep us ahead of the game, and letting us know who is snitching and that type of stuff.

Also there's a narcotic cop who wants to be down on the team with us, too. They both want 2,000 thousand a month for their information and they won't be going thru any of us. They'll be going thru the youngbul C. One cop already provided us with some vital information about some youngbul that works the block for Sahih. His name is Lil Don. Plus, he said that the Feds are interested in making a case on us. They are trying to get us with the R.I.C.O. charge. We haven't decided what to do yet. That's why I came straight to you for advice first. I already decided on what I think should happen."

"Well Nieem, this is an important decision... On one hand, you can get good information about what's going on. Now, first can we trust these cops? Did they show any statement the young man made?" asked Saleem.

"C said he read the statement of Lil Don about only drug dealing."

"Now second, is the statement authentic? Just think, could this be a trick by the police to go kill the young man? Then turn around and put all of y'all under surveillance and catch a murder or an attempted murder on camera? Could they be just using this Lil Don as a pawn? Me personally I say don't deal with the cops. Everybody has been doing fine without them and at the end of the day, they are cops and when shit hits the fan, they're going to snitch on everything they know. Now Lil Don, if he was involved in any murders or what-so-ever, then you can't chance it; he has to go. But if he only knows about drugs and that sort of stuff, I say don't kill him. Try to talk to him, or pay him off. Its one thing to kill a snitch and it's another thing to kill a Federal witness. Now, if he is killed, then guess who knows where it came from? The Homicide Detective... What's going to happen when the cops start wanting more money and y'all don't want to pay them?

These cops are always going to have an advantage over y'all, if y'all kill this young man; you know that, don't you? I say wait it out. If the Feds do come and indict everybody for drugs so what? That comes with the game. We sell drugs and if we get caught, we go to jail and do our time. Come home and get money all over again. That's what I say, but when them murders come into play, that's when them life sentences come, and the death penalty and stuff like that," Saleem finally ended.

"Yeah Unc, I agree with you one hundred percent... I just hope they agree with me."

"Hey, if they don't, you know what you gotta do. Start cleaning up your tracks. You caught a lot of bodies with some of those people. Don't let them bring us down, Nieem." Saleem told me with a serious look.

"Saleem, that's all I really came past for, to put you down with that. I'm about to go back and holla at these niggas. See you later on, or tomorrow, or something... As-Salaam-Alaikum," I said, then turned to go.

"Wa-Alaikum-As-Salaam," Saleem said while I was walking out.

When I got back into my truck, I was just thinking about what the Old Man said to me and I agree with him one hundred percent.

◆　　◆　　◆

Later on that night we all met up around Boyle Street. We still had the block open and all the youngbuls was out there grinding.

Sahih, Shaheed and me, went to the side of the street to talk.

"So, what Saleem say? I didn't have a chance to go holla at him," Sahih asked.

"He told me to leave that shit alone and let everything play out."

"So what, we going to sit around and wait to go to jail?" asked Shaheed.

"Naw, I think we should just shut down shop, for like a month or two, or move everything around the store; fire all the workers and replace them with new one's... Matter of fact, to keep it real. I already told all the workers that this was their last day," I informed them.

"It sounds good. I'm trying to play it safe, because I ain't trying to kill youngbul, only because the cop will know that it came from us directly," said Sahih.

"Sahih, Saleem said the same thing. It ain't like we won't kill a fuckin' snitch, it's just that the police already know where it's coming from, if we kill him," I told them.

"Also, I put Young'in and C on Lil Don, just to shake him up a little bit, not to kill him," Sahih spoke up.

◆　　◆　　◆

Meanwhile, Young'in, C and Lil Don was in the living room of C's house around Park Terrace.

They were smoking weed and talking about fuckin' different bitches.

Suddenly, Lil Don said "that's why I fuck's wit y'all buls... Y'all get bitches and y'all kill a mutha fucka in a minute."

"Hoool homz, you know we ain't on that type of time... We don't be killing shit," said C defensively.

"Come on, stop fronting, I remember when y'all told me about Rell getting rocked. C you told me that Young'in rocked the bul. You probably don't remember, because you was all drunk and shit," Lil Don laughed.

C pulled his gun out. "Nigga, I didn't tell you shit like that. You got me fucked up... Matter of fact homz let me check your ass for a wire, cause you talking real crazy in here."

"Ah man, I ain't got no wire on C, why you trying to play me like that. I would never try to set you niggas up on no police shit," said Lil Don.

Just as Lil Don finished explaining his self. Young'in jumped up, gun in hand and said, "look Don, either you going to let us search you, or your ass will be floating in the Delaware River tonight."

"Okay, okay you can search me." Lil Don said, while throwing his hands up.

As soon as Lil Don said that, the police kicked in the door.

C ran towards the kitchen.

Young'in grabbed Lil Don by the shirt and used him as a shield, while shooting at the cops the whole time.

The first two cops that ran in the house were shot dead soon after they came thru the door.

The others cops that followed shot Young'in and Lil Don both in the head. C, on the other hand, saw Young'in laying on the ground dead and the police were just shooting and coming closer and closer to hitting him in the kitchen.

C lived on the bottom floor and the kitchen had a window so, he shot at it two times and jumped through, only to meet the other cops outside. As soon as he tried to get up and run. He was shot twice in the chest.

◆　◆　◆

Me, Shaheed, and Sahih were all on Boyle Street when we saw all the police zooming past us going straight to Park Terrace. I told them, "I hope they didn't kill Lil Don. If so we are in a world of trouble. As a matter of fact, I'm the fuck outta here."

"Shit, I'm out too... Let's take a ride down A.C. We'll find out what happened later," Sahih said.

We headed down A.C. to just chill and lay low for the rest of the day. That's when Evon called me.

"What's up baby?"

"Nieem, where are you?"

"Down A.C., why what's up?"

"Young'in dead, Young'in dead!" Evon started to cry.

"What?"

"Young'in got killed by the police. They ran in C house and killed Young'in and Lil Don. C tried to jump out of the window and got shot two times in the chest. Also, two cops are dead," Evon carried on.

"Damn, you serious?"

"Would I be sitting here on the phone crying, if I was playing? I'm standing outside looking at the crime scene. They haven't brought Young'in and them out, yet. I just seen the two cops they brought out... Damn baby, I'm scared. What's going on?" She asked.

"I don't know; let me make a couple calls. I'll call you back." I hung up the phone with Evon and told Shaheed and Sahih, Young'in and Lil Don got killed by the police and C got hit twice in the chest. "Plus two cops got killed... My girl just called and told me."

"Damn, Young'in dead! What the fuck happened in that house tonight? We got to lay low until we find out what happened," said Sahih.

Chapter 17

We all stayed the night in Atlantic City, just to be on the safe side. The next day I called home and got word about what went down and found out it was cool to come back. After I dropped off everybody, I went past the store to holla at Saleem. He was behind the counter, reading a paper. He saw me, and just started shaking his head. "As-Salaam-Alaikum, Unc."

"Wa-Alaikum-As-Salaam, Nieem... Did you read the paper?"

"Naw, what they saying?"

"It says 'during an undercover investigation, informant Donald Baker was killed by the Chester Police along with a Young Gunz Drug trafficking member, Ali Wilson, and two Chester City Police Officers were killed during the raid.

One defendant, Eric Brown survived the shoot-out with the police after diving thru a kitchen window and being shot twice in the chest. The defendant Eric Brown had on a bullet proof vest, which saved his life. Currently, Eric Brown is in custody at the Delaware County Jail with no bail, and is being charged with four murders relating from the shoot-out with the police and the intimidation of an informant.

At the time of the undercover investigation Donald Baker had a body wire on trying to help the Chester Police get information from the Notorious Young Gunz'.

Nieem, what made y'all send them boys around there with lil Don? Y'all know how them two are," said Saleem.

"Unc, they weren't supposed to kill him... Sahih sent them around there, just to shake him up a little, not to kill him. They was in C house, so you know they wasn't trying to kill him. Anyway the police killed him."

"Yeah, probably after they threaten to kill him. Damn Nieem, y'all hot now. Y'all got to fall back a little bit... This damn Lil Don had a wire on, and who the hell knows what they got on them wire taps.

They probably got us under surveillance and our phones tapped. I hope you don't talk business over the phone," Saleem said, looking pissed off.

"Naw Saleem, I been stopped all that dumb shit... We should be straight. I don't know what Sahih and Shaheed been doing, though."

"Well, let them both know, don't say anything on them phones and that it is a must y'all shut that block down. So, did you check on C's people and see what's up with him? Make sure you personally send him five hundred dollars and get him a lawyer, immediately. Even though he might be booked solid, but then again I don't see how they can give him four bodies, if he didn't kill them with the gun he had. The cops admitted in the paper that they killed Young'in and Lil Don. We just got to worry about if he killed those two cops. If he did, they will try to give him the death penalty," said Saleem.

"What lawyer you think I should get him?"

"Go to Mark Crunch. With the right money, he can make a lot of shit disappear. That's how I beat that State Racketeering case I had five years ago. Mr. Crunch paid the judge and prosecutor off. That mess costed me one hundred and fifty thousand, but my freedom has no price on it. If I had to pay a million dollars to stay out of jail I would. When you go there, tell him I sent you. He should be able to help C, in-sha Allah. But the million dollar question is, do you think that he will flip on you?" Saleem questioned.

"Naw, that's my youngbul. I don't think he'll go out like that."

"Well, we'll see!" Saleem said, unsurely.

"Yup, we will Unc, but I'm going to still need some work for my people down Delaware."

"Ae man, like I told you, it's better to be patient and see where this go, instead of getting thrown in on a conspiracy for some bullshit ass two or three bricks, and a hundred pounds. Besides, you don't know if them cops been following you down Delaware or not. Who knows, they might have pictures of y'all together down there, so just be easy right now. Go handle that with C first, and then we'll see how to move from there," said Saleem.

"Well. Unc, I'm going to get on top of that today. You think he'll be in there after four o'clock tonight, because I got to go all the way to Delaware to grab some money."

"Yeah, he should be there... Mr. Crunch don't usually leave the office until seven o'clock at night."

"Aight Unc, I'm going to holla at you later. Salaam-Alaikum."

"Wa-Alaikum-As-Salaam, Nieem. Ae, be smart out there. Stay away from the bull shit," Saleem advised.

"Aight."

◆　　◆　　◆

When I left the store I headed straight to the house down Delaware. I walked in the house to see my son Aziz and Mira in front of the T.V.

"Hey baby, you aight? Come and give me a kiss," Mira said.

"I'm good. You hear about what happened last night?"

"Yup, that's why I'm not going crazy about you not coming home. That's a shame they did that to them. Now, you see why I be so scared when you're up there? Everybody kill around that bitch. Cops and all. You talk to C yet?"

"Naw, not yet. I'm about to go holla at a lawyer for him, though. Why don't you come with me, then we can go get something to eat afterwards."

"Okay." Mira said getting up.

"Come here boy, give ya Dad a kiss," I said grabbing my baby boy.

After taking a shower and grabbing fifty thousand for the lawyer, we jumped up in her X5. An hour later we were in the lawyer's reception area, before a young lady sitting behind a desk.

"Hello, may I help you sir?" She asked politely.

"Yes, I'm here to see Mr. Crunch."

"Please have a seat." The women offered.

After waiting for five minutes in the small waiting room, the secretary said "excuse me sir, but you and your wife may go back to see Mr. Crunch."

"Thank you ma'am," I told her, then headed in the direction her hand was pointing to.

Mr. Crunch was a medium size white man with a full head of black hair, wearing a tailor made suit, looking to be in his late thirties. I extended my hand and at the same time saying, "Hello Mr. Crunch, my name is Nieem and this is my fiancée Ms. Thomas."

He shook both of our hands. "It's nice to meet the both of you and what a beautiful baby you have," Mr. Crunch said, smiling.

"Thank you," Mira said.

"So, what can I do for such a beautiful couple?"

"Well Mr. Crunch, I have a friend by the name of Eric Brown, who is charged with four murders. My Uncle Saleem told me that you was the best at handling these types of situations."

"Well, Mr. Brown was just in the paper this morning. I read about what they charged him with. Off the top, I can at least get two murders charges dropped, because if, and I say if the paper was telling the correct story, then they can't charge him with them two murders that the Cops committed. Also, I see they charged him with first degree murder. I don't know if he was the one who killed them cops or not, but if he did, first degree is the wrong charge to give him. I would suggest that, if anything it would be third degree murder. For the simple reason of it not being premeditated, so the most your friend is looking at is twenty years, max. Now, if you want me to take this case, I need a twenty-five thousand retainer, before I look or read any paper work and I want one-hundred thousand for the whole case, only because Saleem is such a good friend of mine." Mr. Crunch said without flinching.

"Well Mr. Crunch, I brought you fifty thousand cash and I want you to communicate directly with me. I also want to know if you can find out if there are any more informants, and I want you to tell me if my friend ever wants to talk to the cops and cooperate."

"Mr. Nieem you know that type of information is confidential between me and my client, but about whether he wants to talk to the cops or anything, I will need you to come see me personally to discuss that type of information. No disrespect to you Ms. Thomas. I can, however, tell you about the wiretap information, and other information that he provided to the police already. I should get all of that in the discovery, when I take the case. I'll go see Mr. Brown, either tonight, or tomorrow. I want you to stop by next week. I should have some information for you then," said Mr. Crunch.

"Okay then Mr. Crunch, I'm going to let you do your thing. I'll see you next week."

"It was nice to meet you two. Please have a nice day!"

◆　◆　◆

After the meeting with the lawyer, me and Mira went to Red Lobster and got something to eat, then went past my mom house. I was trying to spend some family time with her, because lately I been ripping and running the streets. After we left my mom's house, we went back to Delaware. I told her I had to make a run, and left the house.

So many things was going thru my mind. Mr. Crunch, kind of brought me a little comfort, though. I'm glad my man is not going to have to spend the rest of his life in the joint.

The way Mr. Crunch was talking, I know for sure he'd tell me anything I needed to know. Whether C would tell, or if there is still an ongoing investigation.

I'm just going to chill and play the house for a minute, until I see what's up with Mr. Crunch and what type of information he come up with. Riding around Delaware I decided to go see what's up with my man Khalil, all the while thinking about Young'in getting killed. I wonder when he's going to have his Janazah. He's Muslim, so it probably will be within a day or so.

My brain was just racing, when I pulled up on 2-4 and saw my man Khalil out there. I pulled the truck over, jumped out and headed to the porch, where he was sitting, "Khalil, what's up Homz?"

"Nieem, I'm chilling Ock. How everything been wit you and the family?" Khalil asked.

"My man Young'in just got killed by the police last night and my youngbul C locked up for killing two cops, so shit been kind of crazy for me."

"Damn, my man Young'in got killed huh? That's fucked up. Sorry to hear about that shit man," Khalil said looking disappointed.

"That's why I came down to holla at you, 'cause I'm going to be falling back for a minute, until I find out what's going on. When Young'in got killed an informant got killed with him and he had a wire on. So I'm just putting you down, 'cause they was investigating me and my squad. I don't know if the police been following me or what. I got somebody on top of it right now, though, so I should know something real soon."

"So, you think that they might got us on surveillance?" said Khalil.

"Naw, you know they can't see through no houses, or thru no cars or nothing like that, so the only thing that they will have us two doing is meeting each other and shaking hands and shit like that."

"I'm still going to be on point out here, you feel me! But damn, I had something for you. I got something lined up next week." Khalil said, while shaking his head.

"What you got lined up?" I asked a bit eagerly.

"Remember that college girl that I was fuckin'?

Well anyway, she turned me on to a check cashing place she work at. Babe said that on Friday mornings she be counting one hundred thousand in cash that be in the safe; and it only be her and two other cashiers and one manager in the store.

They all come to work at around 7:30am," said Khalil.

"Can she be trusted?"

"I think so."

"What if the bitch start acting all scary when the police question her, because you know they are going to question her, right?"

"Yeah, I know." Khalil replied, seeming not to care.

"Okay then, you got to give me your word. If I feel like this girl is a liability to us, you're going to be the one that kill her. It's too much on the line for us robbing a check cashing store and take a chance at this girl telling on us." I said seriously, then went on to ask, "where she from anyway, and is she a street girl?"

"Ae Nieem, I would never play you like that. I definitely will kill her myself, if I see any weakness in the broad. Plus, she live up Concord Ave., but go to school down Delaware State College and yeah she grew up in the hood. Her Dad use to get money back in the day, before he got caught up in a conspiracy wit the bul Jayvon and them," said Khalil.

"So how you want to do this?" I asked.

"I went and checked the spot out already. Where the back door is, there are no cameras in the area. Not from what I've seen. They arrive at separate times, but before 7:30am. I seen it for myself. The manager comes in at 7:00am and at 7:15am the armored truck drops the money off, or pick it up from the day before. I don't know exactly what it does and she don't either, but I've seen the armored truck at 7:15 on Friday mornings for the past three weeks. Now, each cashier comes in separately. My girl be coming in like 7:20. That will be the perfect way to get in there.

When we get inside, that's when we got to worry about security cameras, because it's one as soon as you walk into the back door. She said when you come in from the back door the safe is to the left, in the manager's office. He is the only one with the combination, but most of the time it be unlocked, because it's all girls working there and the neighborhood it's in is not that bad."

"Ae, Khalil I'm trusting you on this one, and I'm going with your judgment. Who else is going wit us?"

"Just me and you. I didn't trust nobody else. I got a couple of young wild cowboys, but they will go in there drawing and shit trying to kill a mutha fucka, on some bull shit," Khalil replied.

"I'm wit it. So, when and where?"

"We're going to do it Friday, at around 7:15. The Check Cashing place is in Newark, so we going to leave from here like 6:30 and just sit and watch everything play out.

One thing I'm going to need you to get is the guns. We need two AK's, just in case we get trouble coming out," Khalil suggested.

"I can take care of that."

"So, it's on then?"

"Where we going to meet at?"

"Around the corner at my spot. Meet me there at 6:00 a.m."

"I'll be there wit the guns... If the plan changes, call me. Well I'm going to get at you later; I got to make a run."

"Aight, Nieem," Khalil said giving me dap.

Chapter 18

Young'in had a nice Islamic Janazah; a lot of people came and paid their respects. It was Friday morning and I was on my way to make this move with my man Khalil. Now, if my squad knew that I was going down here to rob a fuckin' check cashing place, they would think I'm fuckin' crazy, because we rob drug dealers not businesses and shit like that. Plus, we don't know if the police is watching us or not.

◆   ◆   ◆

An hour later me and Khalil were sitting in the mini-van, looking at the armored truck pull up.

"Everything on time like I told you Nieem. Look at your clock, it's 7:15 a.m." Khalil said with much pride.

"Yeah, so far, so good," I told him. We were parked in between a truck and a car, in back of the check cashing store, which is shared with the employees of a computer store that don't open until 8:00 a.m.

"Nieem, here we go baby. She pulling up in that blue Honda Accord. You ready?"

"Do or die nigga, let's get it." Khalil pulled up and as soon as I saw her opening the door I jumped out of the van, with the AK pointed at her, she was down with the whole twist, so of course she didn't scream. I was really impressed by the terrified look she put on. I pushed her through the door, and she fell on the floor. What a good actress, she was. "Everybody put your hands on your fuckin' head, and lay on the floor!" I yelled at them.

Shock was written on all of their faces as they followed the order. I grabbed the manager. Khalil came behind me and started gathering the girls up and putting handcuffs on them. I took the manager in his office, and like the girl said, the safe was already open. I told the manager wit the AK pointed at him to put all the money in a trash bag that I pulled out of my pocket.

After he put all the money in the bag, I waved Khalil over to bring the girls in to lock everybody in the manager's office. Before exiting through the back door Khalil broke the phone jack off the wall, so they couldn't make any calls, then we left out the back door and rode off without any trouble.

We made it back to Khalil's house around 8:30 in the morning. We sat down and counted the money, and it was ninety thousand dollars. I took forty thousand; Khalil took the same, which left ten thousand for the girl. I chilled up in his spot, until it was time for me to go holla at the lawyer, Mr. Crunch. Last night I was wit Shaheed and Sahih and they both gave me some money for the lawyer. I told them that I would get wit them, after I talked to him.

◆　　◆　　◆

It was 4:00 p.m. when I walked in Mr. Crunch's office. "Hello. How may I help you?" The Secretary asked in her pleasant voice.

"Yes, I have an appointment to see Mr. Crunch. Is he in?"

"Yes sir. Please have a seat, and he will be right with you."

In less than two minutes, the secretary directed me back to his office. When I stepped in, Mr. Crunch extended his hand, which I accepted.

"Mr. Nieem, how are you?"

"I'm hanging in there Mr. Crunch."

"Well, so far everything looks good. I got most of the discovery. The informant provided information about a person by the name of Sahih Muhammad. Do you know him?"

"Yeah."

"Well anyway, it's nothing important and since the informant got killed in the shoot-out, they won't be able to use none of the statements he provided."

"Did the informant talk about any murders?" I asked, hoping that wasn't the case.

"No, he said the workers are never allowed to be involved in stuff like that. Also, there are no pending investigations on the so called 'Young Gunz' and the Feds were never involved in the case. Now, I met with C last night. He told me to tell you what's up and to come see him if you can get out to the jail. Besides that, he has a preliminary hearing in two weeks and I talked to the prosecutors who'll be dropping two charges against him. The murder of the informant Donald Baker and the murder of Ali Wilson. The prosecutors said they are pressing the two other murder charges, which are the cop killings. The ballistics tests hasn't come back yet, but when they do, like I told C, they'll get dismissed too, because C said he didn't shoot at all and that he had a 45 Smith and Wesson," said Mr. Crunch.

"Mr. Crunch, what was the reason the police raided the house?"

"Their justification was because the informant had been asked to be checked for a wire."

"So, is C going to be charged for threatening to kill him?"

"He's already charged with that. It's just worded different, but I think I might be able to get that beat at trial, because Ali Wilson said that he would kill the informant not C." Mr. Crunch said confidently.

"Okay that sounds good... Oh yeah, before I forget. Remember when I had my fiancé in, and I asked could you let me know if C decided to testify, to tell me. And you responded that you'll talk to me one on one and that, that type of information could get you disbarred?"

"I said that because I didn't know who you were at the time. Now, that I did some research, I would surely work with you in anyway," said Mr. Crunch.

"I understand quite well what you are saying," I responded.

"Well is there anything else you wanted to know about the case?"

"No. I'm going to have the rest of the money for you, after the preliminary hearing. Tell C I said what's up and that I'll send somebody up there to support him, because I can't be in there with all them cops during the hearing."

"Okay then, I'll talk to you later, Mr. Nieem."

After the meeting with Mr. Crunch, a lot of stress was lifted. I was on my way to holla at Sahih and let him know about everything and that we can open the block back up. Pulling in front of his apartment in Philly, I saw his 500 Benz parked in the complex. I jumped out of the truck, and after a couple of knocks, he opened the door, looking anxious.

"So, what did the lawyer say?" Sahih wasted no time asking.

"He said that there is no investigation on us, anymore, and that Lil Don was the only witness cooperating with them and the wire he wore ain't have nothing, because that was Lil Don's first time wearing it."

"Damn, that's good to hear." Sahih said exhaling a deep breath.

"We can open the block back up," I told him.

"You holla at Saleem and tell him about what the lawyer said?"

"Naw, not yet. I came straight to tell you because the bul was trying to line you up."

"Yeah, I feel you."

"Where ya brother at?"

"I haven't heard from him since last night, when we all was together. So, what you got planned for the day, soldier?" Sahih asked.

"I'm going to holla at my Unc in a minute, and then I'm going up the way to see what's going on?"

"Ae Nieem, I'm about to get dressed and all of that. Tell Saleem I'm coming past a little later."

"Aight, I'm gone." I told Sahih as I headed out the door.

On my way down to Chester, I drove in silence trying collect my thoughts. Suddenly, my phone rung to life on the passenger's seat.

"Yo, what's up?" I answered, after looking at the unfamiliar number on the display.

"Nieem, what the fuck is up cuz?" said Lil Nigga, whose voice couldn't be mistaken.

"Oh shit! Where you at nigga?"

"I just got out today. What's good wit you?"

"Ae man, you know me, just trying to get some mutha fuckin' paper."

"Nieem, y'all niggas names be ringing bells up in the joint. Man, I heard about what happened to Young'in. I was fucked up 'bout that. You know C, was up there wit me. I had to calm him down a couple times. He be 'bout to crush niggas for anything. Where you at?" Lil Nigga asked.

"On my way back from Philly. Where you at, so I can come grab you real quick?"

"I'm down on 5th Street, at my baby mom's spot. It's right around the corner from the projects."

"Give me fifteen minutes."

"What kind of car you in?"

"A Yukon truck."

"Aight then!" Lil Nigga said, then disconnected.

'Damn Lil Nigga home', I thought. His real name is Jihad. Him and my Uncle Saleem son got the same name. Lil Nigga is my Uncle Saleem step-son. Unc married his mom when he was six months old and we had been close ever since I could remember. Lil Nigga just did two years in the county jail for a probation violation, but was originally locked up for something way more serious.

Like two years ago, Lil Nigga killed this bul named Fat Cat. The bul was running around the city talking shit about how he was going to rob him, but the real issue was that Fat Cat's girl was fuckin' Lil Nigga on the low and she told Fat Cat she didn't want him no more. So, Fat Cat was telling everybody that would listen that he was going to grab Lil Nigga and rob him.

I stepped to him about the rumor and he told me that people was lying and that he would never try anything like that, but Lil Nigga was heading home one night and noticed a car following him. Instead of going home, he kept it moving and called Young'in and C telling them the description of the car. Young'in told him who it was that was driving it because they seen him earlier that day. Suddenly, Fat Cat stopped following. When Fat Cat turned off, Lil Nigga went and laid at Fat Cat girl's house, and when he pulled up and got out of the car to go, Lil Nigga jumped out of the bushes and hit him up.

Fat Cat's girl saw the whole thing. Lil Nigga got away that night, but police locked him up the next day. He got rid of all the clothes and gun the same night of the murder; which left only the girl in the window. I went and paid her ten thousand, not to show up in court, then I had Young'in take pictures of her daughter at school and mail them to her house. The girl never testified, and the murder was dismissed at the first hearing, but Lil Nigga had violated his probation by submitting a hot urine.

I pulled up in front of the house and beeped the horn three times. My little cuz came running out of the house, dressed in an all black Pelle Pell leather jacket, an a black fitted hat, Rocka wear jeans, and some wheat timbs.

"Nieem, what's up cuz? I love you nigga. I missed the hell out of you," Lil Nigga said as he embraced me.

"I missed you too, cuz. A lot of shit been going on since you been down."

"Yeah, I was fucked up about Face, but when I heard you took care of that shit, I was like yeah nigga, big cuz a fuckin' gun...

Niggas out the jawn, scared to death of y'all buls, they know y'all 'bout business. Plus y'all 'bout getting money. I was proud to say that I was ya peoples."

"So what you trying to do cuz? I need you to run the block up the way," I added before Lil Nigga could answer.

"Damn right Nieem. I need to get this money. I'll run that bitch." Lil Nigga answered without hesitation.

"You know Young'in use to run it, but it been shut down for like a week for some bull shit that went down. I was going to open it up, after I holla at Saleem; did you get at him yet?"

"I seen him earlier. I went past the store. We had a long talk about a lot of shit. He told me everything goes thru you on the weed and powder," said Lil Nigga.

"Well, I'll probably open the block up tomorrow because I was going to holla at Saleem today, but you called me and I know he probably left the store, by now. Yeah, though, I'm definitely going to let you run the block... It's still the same as usual. Sahih and Shaheed got the boy out there and I got everything else. I'm going to hire the old workers back. Them youngbuls will be out there tomorrow. You already know all of them... You get some pussy yet?"

"You know I got that earlier, nigga. I'm a mutha fuckin' bitch catcher. Yo, I heard you had two youngbuls. How are they doing and how is wifey doing?" said Lil Nigga.

"They all good... Why you ain't go holla at her ya self? I know you went and seen her cousin that you was fuckin'."

"Naw, I'm going to holla at everybody tomorrow. I was thinking about going over A.C. tonight." said Lil Nigga.

"What you got a rental car already?"

"Yeah, I got one parked up the Gardens. Saleem got it for me, Nieem drop me off up the way, so I can get wit this babe that was riding wit me. She from Philly. This bul, who was my celly for like a year, turned me on to her. Thrull-nigga; he get out next month. We suppose to do some big things together. He said he got peoples from Southwest Philly and that they getting some major change. But the Philly girl is bad as shit. I might take her down A.C. wit me. Ae Nieem, I think she the one," Lil Nigga was all smiles while saying this.

"Damn, she got you open already and you ain't even fucked her yet. That's crazy man," I replied, all the while shaking my head.

"Yeah, whatever nigga. I been down two years and that phone sex, and them letters she was sending got a nigga open, for real. Plus, my car parked over there Ock, behind the jeep right there," Lil Nigga said pointing across my chest.

"The Lincoln Towncar right there?" I asked.

"Yeah. I'm good right here cuz. I'll holla at you tomorrow."

"Meet me down the store, in the afternoon, because I got to holla at Saleem."

"Aight. I'll be there waiting for you," Lil Nigga said heading out my truck.

Chapter 19

Last night I stayed around my apartment with Evon and my son Tarik. Evon got up early, fixed me and Tarik some breakfast, then after an hour of running around, he took a nap. Evon and me was in the bed half of the morning catching up from me not being around, me and Evon got a good fuck session in and a little followed. Around noon time, I gave her and my son a kiss goodbye and was on my way.

The first thing I did was call Mira to let her know that I was handling some real important business last night, and that I'm alright. Mira don't question me when I tell her stuff like that because she know what type of business I'm into, and understands what comes with being a hustler's wife.

Shaheed called earlier, telling me to come pass the way, after I holla at my peoples. He said it was something important that he had to tell me.

Up at Ameer's I entered thru the back of the store, where I see Lil Niggas rental car was parked.

I gave my Salaams to everybody in the back of the store.

"As-Salaam-Alaikum, Nieem." Saleem said, as I came inside.

"Wa-Alaikum-As-Salaam," I replied.

"How you been? And how are the boys?" Unc asked.

"Everything been aight wit me and the boys are doing good. I was just wit little Tarik. That boy bad as shit. All he wants to do is fight and get into everything."

"Ha, Ha, Ha. Boys are going to be boys. Did you see your knucklehead cousin, yet?"

"I seen him last night. Where he at? I see his car out back."

"He went to the Rite-Aid for me. He'll be back any minute, so, did you get wit the lawyer yet?" Saleem asked.

"I talked to him yesterday. When I was coming over here to tell you what he said, Lil Nigga called me, and we was together for awhile.

But the lawyer said everything is good. No investigations or nothing; C's going to be good. They're dropping two murders, and may drop the other two when the tests from the crime scene and all that junk come back."

"That sounds good. You can open the block back up now, huh?"

"Yup, that's what I was going to tell you. I need some work."

"I got something here for somebody else, but I'm going to go ahead and give it to you."

"How much is it?"

"Ten bricks." Saleem answered, while moving past me with a box in his hand.

"I'm going to need some weed, too."

"I'll have that tomorrow."

"Unc, I'm going to let Lil Nigga run the block."

"I don't know why y'all call him that. That bul name is Jihad," Saleem said shaking his head. "It's cool. I just hope he got some sense. After being in jail for two years. Hopefully, he don't start acting like some wild cowboy."

Just then, Lil Nigga walked in the store with a Rite-Aid bag in hand. He came over to the table, where we were.

"What's up cuz?" He said to me.

"What's good wit you?"

"What I tell both of you? When you see a Muslim, you give him the greetings of Peace... I know both of you are doing all type of other things that's against Islam, but when you two are amongst me... Y'all are going to greet each other like Muslims," Saleem said with force.

"Abu (father) you right. That's my fault." Lil Nigga said, apologetically. "I'm going to start giving the greetings from now on."

"Me too Unc, my bad," I chipped in.

Turning to Lil Nigga, I asked "what's up cuz? What you do last night?"

"I went and stayed up Philly with that girl. I was telling you about," he answered.

"She got any friends or sisters for me," I asked, jokingly.

"Man, that girl got a whole squad of chicks she be wit. All of them pretty as hell, too. Last night a couple of them was in there, and they was on my dick. I was going to call you to come over, but I know you're sucker-for-love ass was in the spot with one of ya wifeys," Lil Nigga shot a low blow. Then turned to Saleem. "Abu, what you doing after work?"

"I got a couple of runs to make. Why, what's up Jihad?" Saleem inquired.

"Naw, I was just asking. I wanted you to go down A.C. wit me tonight," Lil Nigga answered.

"Jihad I don't be going down A.C. no more. That place is rigged down there. I learnt, never go against the house because they always win," Saleem said.

"Aight then, I'm going to grab some Sixer tickets for me, you and Nieem. I'm trying to go see them bust the Lakers ass," Lil Nigga came back with.

"Now, that sounds good... I'm wit going to see my team play," Saleem said excitedly.

"Ae Unc, won't you grab that for me. So, I can get moving. Plus, I know you about to open the store!"

Without a word, Saleem left to go grab something.

"Lil Nigga, what's up man, you coming up the way? I'm trying to open the block up today."

"Nieem, I'm going to stay with Abu for another hour, so I'll be up there later."

"Don't be all day. I know you trying to get some fuckin' paper."

Saleem walked back over to us carrying two Gucci bags. "Nieem, take them jawns out of the box and put that work in these bags. I already told you what it is... We'll talk about the price tomorrow."

"Aight then, I'm going to go take care of some business Unc. Ae Jihad, make sure you get wit me as soon as you leave here. It's been shut down for a week now. So, I'm trying to get back all that clientele we use to have."

"I told you I got you," said Lil Nigga.

"Salaam Alaikum," I told them.

"Wa-Alaikum-As-Salaam," Saleem and Lil Nigga said together.

◆　◆　◆

I left the store and went straight up to Killa Hill. I took nine bricks and put them in my safe around on Park Terrace and took the other brick around this junkie house. I got one of my other workers around there that's in charge of bagging up the work now.

While he was doing that, I was sitting in the chair smoking a bag of weed waiting on Shaheed to come through and holla at me.

I saw him when I picked the youngbul up from around the store. Shaheed was at the pay phone, waiting for a call.

He said afterwards, he would come around and talk to me.

Twenty minutes later Shaheed was knocking on the back door. I went and let him in.

"Nieem, what's up?"

"I can't call it big fella. What's good wit you?"

"I'm good... Step in the kitchen wit me right quick, so I can holla at you," said Shaheed.

We headed for the kitchen, "me and the bul Kasul from over the Eastside was talking last night. I seen him up in the Cherry Hill Mall over in Jersey. He was asking me about all of us getting together and taking the city by siege. Like, what he was saying I was feeling, because you know that's the same thing me, you and my brother been talking about for the longest," Shaheed said further.

"Yeah, we been talking about it, but what about Kasul? You think we can trust the bul?"

"Now, that's a different story. He said he wanted to holla at us about that shit that happened wit C and Young'in... Anyway though, we should think real hard about this. How he broke it down to me was, that everybody from the Eastside, Crosby Squares, niggas up in the Farms, Middletown, and 8th Street would have to get work from him and his people. And everybody from the William Penn Projects, Bennett, the whole 3rd Street and McCafferty Village, must get there work from us. Kasul said, he has a vicious hit squad for the niggas that don't want to go along with the plan, and you already know what we about so, we might as well organize this shit and get some money," Shaheed said with much emphasis.

"It sounds good, but I'm loyal to my Uncle and he supplies half of the niggas in the city, so it would be easier to move everything thru me, but I don't know if Saleem will go wit that," I told Shaheed.

"Kasul said he already got a plug that will give him the work he needs... He also said that he knows that we ain't going to stop fuckin' wit Saleem."

"Yeah, I know that too." I said, interrupting Shaheed. "So did you holla at your brother yet?"

"I told him already... He said he wit it, if we all agree. I told Sahih to come down here, so we can all talk about it."

"And when are we going to holla at Kasul?"

"Tonight at the Christian Mall, down Delaware, I told him to meet us in the food court, at eight o'clock. That's why we all need to get together first," Shaheed answered.

"Yeah, I feel you. I'm wit it, but out of respect for my Uncle, I'm going to put him down wit what's going on."

"I feel exactly what you saying." Shaheed shot back.

"Are y'all opening the block today, or what?"

"Sahih is down at Saleem's, now. We about to open up as soon as he comes back wit the work. I got all the youngbuls lined up waiting already. I heard Lil Nigga came home last night. Sahih put him on the phone when he was in Ameer's." Shaheed ended.

"I got him running the block for me."

"You better tell that nigga don't be too rough on them youngbuls. You know he can get kind of crazy out that jawn," Shaheed replied.

"Lil Nigga calmed down."

"Yeah, I feel you. So, how long are you going to be in here?" Shaheed asked.

"Not too long," I answered and walked out of the kitchen and into the dining room, where the youngbul was busy at work.

He bagged up a couple ounces in twenties, which was more than enough for right now, we gathered everything up and then me, him and Shaheed left the house.

Up on Boyle Street I opened the block myself. My youngbul was doing all the hand to hand sales. And I was just out there to watch everything go smooth. After every five hundred pack he sold. I took the money and gave him more work.

We were sitting out there for like two hours. And money really started coming when the junkies saw me out there.

Lil Nigga and Sahih had pulled up on the block, and I took Lil Nigga to the side.

"What's up cuz?"

"I just left the store with Abu. I see you got everything moving out here."

"Yeah, you was taking too long... So, you ready?"

"How you want me to do it?"

"All the work is in that abandon house right there. The wooden door isn't nailed on there, so all you got to do is pick it up and move it to the side. It's got nine ounces in there that's not bagged up. The rest of the work in there is bagged up already, in five hundred packs. That's stashed in the oven. If you run out, there's more work in the house over there wit the young jawn Kia. You already know her; I already told her you'll be coming to get some shit from her. Plus, it's a gun in the oven, and one on top of the car tire in the yard. Anything else you need to know?"

"Naw, I'm cool. I got everything under control. How long you normally keep the block open?" Lil Nigga asked.

"Until like eleven o'clock, but it's up to you."

"Aight then, I got this."

After talking to Lil Nigga, I walked over to where Sahih and Shaheed was setting up shop. I fired up a dutch while they got everything together. We had to talk about this shit with Kasul. The plan sounded good, though. I was just wondering to myself, whether we could trust the bul.

Kasul was a sneaky, dangerous nigga. He get money and take money, too. But one thing about him is that, he don't rob no niggas from Chester; only out-of-towners. And like us, his named stayed in some shit. Either it was for shooting a nigga up, or it was a murder that had some connection to him or his team.

Just last week, one of his youngbuls ran up in a barber shop and shot up this bul from over the Eastside that called his babymom a bitch. Kasul is definitely about his business. I personally got to be on point and make sure I stay two steps ahead of this nigga, but first we got to squash that beef. C killed two of his men. This might be a trap for him to kill all three of us at the same time. Still, I'm going to the mall tonight to meet with the nigga though... I want to see this nigga face and body language and see what type of vibe this bul giving off.

"Nieem, what's up homz? I see you over there in deep thought." Sahih said interrupting my thoughts.

"I was just thinking about a couple of things. You know how that weed have a nigga. What's up wit you, though?"

"Ah man, I'm good. I was just at the store wit Saleem and crazy ass Lil Nigga. What you think about that shit wit Kasul?"

"Sahih, I'm wit it, if you niggas wit it. We just got to be ex-tra cautious dealing wit bul."

"I agree one hundred percent, we got to be on point wit the nigga." said Sahih.

"I got to holla at my peoples first, before I jump into this. You feel me?"

"Yeah Ock."

"I'm going wit y'all tonight to holla at the bul, but I'm not going to give an answer, until I holla at my peoples."

"Well, if we decide to make the move, I got somebody that can get us some guns and shit, but they are going to be out of the store," said Shaheed.

"Who?" Sahih asked in a bit of disbelief.

"Cousin Jane," Shaheed answered calmly.

"Shaheed, Cousin Jane is a damn junkie," Sahih responded.

"So, what does that mean?"

"It means that she'll do anything to get high. If Jane gets caught for selling guns, she's going to snitch on your ass," Sahih said, shaking his head.

"Naw mutha fucka, we are going to scratch the numbers off the guns," Shaheed said like he had it all figured out.

"Man look, you do what you do. I'm not buying no guns from her," Sahih stated flatly.

"Me either Ock, I'm cool. That shit too risky, I rather keep getting my shit off the streets from niggas like I always been doing, or I get them from Saleem," I chipped in.

"Y'all two niggas don't got to worry about it then. I'm going to deal with her myself, because you two acting crazy right now," said Shaheed.

"I hope you make sure she don't buy shit for anybody else up here," said Sahih.

"I'm going to break all that shit down to her," Shaheed told his brother.

We all stayed out there just chilling and smoking to let time go by. It was 7:30 p.m. Time to go down to meet Kasul and them. We all took a gun, just in case these niggas was trying to catch us slipping at the mall parking lot.

We rode down to Delaware in silence, for the most part. Everybody was in there own zone. That's when I told them "ae, dig this homz. When we get to the mall, try to park in a well lit area and real close to the mall," I told Sahih and Shaheed.

"Yeah, I feel you Ock," said Sahih.

"Remember, we got to be on point," Shaheed assured.

Finally, we found a nice parking spot right across from the main entrance of the mall. We took our guns in the mall with us because we weren't going to do any shopping. It was strictly business with us... Holla at the bul Kasul in the food court and be out. Shaheed spotted Kasul first. Kasul was a big bald head nigga. He did time Upstate, and while he was up there, all he did was lift weights. He had two of his partners with him. I knew both of them. They were from over the Eastside.

When we got to the table, everybody said what's up, and shook hands. Every time I shake a nigga hand, I make sure that when I hug him, to see if I feel a gun, and each of them did have one. It's understandable though, because they don't know what type of time we was on, so I don't feel disrespected.

Kasul broke the silence. "Did Shaheed tell y'all what I was trying to do?"

"Yeah. We all wit it, but we got to make sure that we can trust each other." said Sahih.

"Sahih, I got no hard feelings about what them youngbuls did to my men. I got over that... I'm about my paper first and foremost." Kasul answered in a sincere manner.

"Kasul I feel you. I'm about my paper, also, and the idea that you came up wit sounds good, but what's going to happen when one of your homies from the Eastside don't agree with the fact that one of us had something to do with getting their family killed, and try to get at one of us?" I asked him.

"Nieem, I will personally kill them myself... All a man got is his word and I promise that what I say, I mean, and I mean what I say. After this day, you'll never have to worry about any back-stabbing from my end. You have in me, a friend until the end, unless you or anybody else cross me first. Then we all know how that goes." said Kasul.

"I agree. So, when you trying to start this thing?" I asked.

"I was hoping real soon, Ock. While we start pulling up on niggas blocks, and pushing up on the so-called connects that run them, I think, and this is just my opinion, that y'all should be doing it at the same time. Niggas in the city going to start panicking when they hear what we're doing, and either they're going to get down, or lay down." Kasul answered with authority.

"Just one thing Kasul. We got our own connect and I got to holla at him first, because he be serving a lot of niggas in the parts of the city that we're going to be pulling up on." I told them.

"I know your Uncle Saleem got half of the city on blast on the low, but niggas won't try to grab him, because of y'all," said Kasul.

"We know that!" said Shaheed.

"If I ever heard a nigga thinking about grabbing my Uncle, I would personally kill the nigga's whole family and that is for a nigga just thinking about it." I said with much emphasis, to make sure my point was understood.

"I feel you Ock. I'm just telling y'all something I heard in my travels. This is one of the reasons why I came at y'all with this idea." Kasul answered honestly.

"I understand," I told Kasul.

"So we can all agree that it's on?" Kasul asked looking at everyone.

"Like I said before Kasul, I'm wit it, but I got to get wit my peoples first. So, by tomorrow I can give everybody my answer."

"I'm wit that... How about you two?"

"I'm wit it, if my man goes along wit it," said Shaheed.

"Same here," said Sahih.

"As soon as you holla at him tomorrow, hit me and let me know what's up." said Kasul.

"Aight."

After everybody shook hands, we made for the exit, and I was on point when we hit the parking lot. Nothing happened, though, so we all rode back up to the Gardens in silence, until we got off the Highland Ave., exit. That's when Sahih said "What y'all think about the meeting?"

"I think he was honest about what he was saying." I told them.

"I do too. I didn't sense any deceit in his tone." Shaheed added.

"Me either. You think Saleem is going to go for this one?" Sahih asked.

"I don't know, but I'm going to try and convince him."

By the time we finished talking about all that just happened down at the mall, Sahih was pulling up on Boyle St. Everything was looking good out there. Lil Nigga was standing in the yard watching the scenery. The junkies were lining up on the side of the street waiting to get served. We all jumped out of my truck and walked over to the yard where Lil Nigga was standing in.

"What's up?" Sahih greeted him.

"Ah man, I can't call it." Lil Nigga said dapping fist with him.

"Police been out here?" Shaheed questioned.

"Yeah, that's why I'm standing in the yard... It looked like they wanted to jump out on me earlier. I had a gun on me too." Lil Nigga replied, seeming unphased.

"Damn, we got these guns on us." said Shaheed.

"We cool in the yard. They can't come up here. Plus I got the door open, if they try to, we can just walk in the house."

"Ae Cuz, let me holla at you for a second." I told Lil Nigga, then pulled him to the side.

"What's up?"

"What you do so far?"

"$3,800.00. It's only 10 o'clock, though. I was thinking about staying out here until the bars close, at 2:30 a.m." said Lil Nigga.

"Cuz, I got some big things in motion, right now. I'm going to need you."

"Nieem, you know I'm here for you... Anything you need me for and that's even if you want me to drop a nigga for you... You know I'm going to ride for my peoples. I love you niggas to death," he assured.

"Well, as soon as I get the okay on everything, I'm going to put you down wit what's going on. This move we trying to make, though, we might have to kill a couple of buls."

"So be it. I'm going all the way wit you cuz. You got my loyalty."

"I'm about to go in for the night. Be careful out here. If you don't sell all of that work in the abandoned crib, put it in the young girl house. See you tomorrow."

"Aight, Cuz" said Lil Nigga.

Chapter 20

I stayed down Delaware wit my baby Mira. I woke up early and was playing with Aziz the whole morning, while Mira got some much needed rest. Aziz is a good little boy. People say that he is my little twin. I'm going to try and start having my sons together, so they can have that brotherly love.

When Mira woke up she cooked us some food, and stuff, then she started getting on my ass about not spending enough time in the house with them. I told her I'm in the middle of trying to make some big things happen, and that I'll make it up to them.

After everything was cool at the crib, I headed down Chester to go to Ameer's. I parked around back, as usual, and made my way behind the counter.

"As-Salaam-Alaikum," Saleem greeted.

"Wa-Alaikum-As-Salaam," I returned.

"I got the rest of that work you wanted in the back," he told me.

"Yeah, I came to grab that but I wanted to holla at you about the bul Kasul."

"What, he on some bull shit again?" Saleem asked with a curious look.

"Naw, we met up last night and squashed all of that, and we all talked about trying to take the whole city over. Me, Sahih, and Shaheed going to have the whole Westside, including the whole 3rd street and Kasul and his squad is going to have the Eastside, plus 8th Street."

"It sounds good if all of these people go along with this little idea of y'alls. But one thing about it is I serve half of these niggas."

"Yeah, I know, that's why I told all of them from the gate that, if my peoples don't agree to it, I'm not fuckin' wit it. Sahih and Shaheed agreed. Their loyalty is to us. So, you get the final call on this issue."

"It sounds good. Y'all three would make a lot more money, but the only thing is the murders that's going to come with this, but I see all of y'all really what this opportunity to do something in the city nobody else every tried." said Saleem.

"Plus, I wanted to ask you to send all the coke thru me and to stop serving these niggas so it can be more easier for us to make this move."

"Yeah, I could take the back seat on this," Unc answered, simply, "I'm trying to be in the cut, anyway," he added.

"So, you giving me the okay?"

"Yeah, but when shit hits the fan from all this killing that is about to happen, I hope you cover your tracks and keep an eye on that nigga Kasul. Seriously, I knew him for a long time. If he fucks wit you, he's going to ride to the end. But if he don't fuck wit you, he can be a dangerous mutha fucka."

"Oh yeah, Unc, when we was down the mall talking yesterday, the bul Kasul said that the only reason niggas won't grab you is because of me and Sahih and them. I told him that if I ever think a nigga was trying to grab you I would kill the nigga whole family, just to make an example for anybody else that would even think about doing some shit like that."

"He said that huh? I ain't worried about none of them chumps. That's why I got sons and nephews. Also, this old man keeps a gun on him.

You just make sure you stay on point." Saleem ended.

"We got to step that weight up, Unc."

"How much you think you can handle?"

"Give me fifty bricks and let me see how long it takes," I told him.

Saleem walked in the back to go get the work that I was already coming to get. "Here you go. I put that weed in there, too."

"Aight then, I'm going to get wit you later. I got to make a couple of moves. As-Salaam-Alaikum."

"Wa-Alaikum-As-Salaam.

◆　◆　◆

I got in my truck and called Sahih and Shaheed, telling them we had the green light. Shaheed said that he was going to go holla at Kasul and let him know what was up. When I hung up wit Shaheed, I called my bul down DE and told them that I was on my way down there. First, I dropped off some work around Park Terrace.

When I got to Delaware, I called my man Khalil, just as I pulled up in front of his crib; I jumped out of the truck with two City Blue bags in my hands. Khalil was waiting on the steps. As soon as I jumped out of the truck, he turned around and went and opened the door to the house.

"Nieem, what's going on wit you?" said Khalil.

"I'm good Ock. How everything been wit you?"

"Ah man, I can't complain." said Khalil.

"I brought six bricks instead of the usual three. From now on whatever you buy, I'm going to front you the same, except the weed," I told him.

"Yeah, that's what's up."

"These six I got right here, I want twenty stacks a piece for them. I want the regular price for the weed," I informed.

"Sounds good to me," Khalil answered happily.

"Khalil I might need you Ock. I'm about to make a couple big moves in the city, and if niggas don't act right, I might have to lay a couple of them out."

"Ae Nieem, you know I got you," Khalil assured.

"I'm going to be getting wit you, though. I got somebody waiting on me."

"Aight then. Just call when you need me."

I made a run around the corner and dropped off the rest of the weed to R. We was sitting on R's people's porch for like an hour or so just talking and bullshitting. I fired up a dutch, while he was telling me about this new chick he had met up Philly. The bul was in love already, and I told him that he was open.

♦ ♦ ♦

I made it back up the way in less than twenty minutes. Lil Nigga and one of Sahih's workers was on the block, so I pulled over.

"Nieem, what's up," Lil Nigga was the first to speak.

"I'm cool, what's up wit you cuz?"

"Trying to get at a dollar," he shot back.

"Yeah, I hear you. Did you see Sahih or Shaheed out here today?"

"Yeah, I seen Shaheed like twenty minutes ago. He went around the store."

"You talk to Saleem today?"

"I went past his house earlier today. We was kicking it for like an hour or so. I try to at least get wit him every day, if I can," said Lil Nigga.

While, Lil Nigga was talking, Shaheed was walking up the street, talking on his phone. By the time he got to us, he hung up, then shook my hand.

"I holla'ed at Kasul already, and told him it was a go."

"So, when are we going to go and let these buls know?" I asked him.

"As soon as Sahih get up here we can go make our rounds. Plus, I just bought two AKs," said Shaheed.

"What, the babe got them for you?" I asked.

"Yeah we went to two different stores."

"Let me hold one of them, just in case a nigga jump out there all crazy."

"I shouldn't let you hold shit... Y'all two niggas didn't want to fuck wit her, but want to use the mutha fuckin' guns. That's crazy."

"Ah man, stop crying." I said jokingly.

"I ain't crying nigga. I'm just keeping it real," Shaheed responded.

While we was waiting for Sahih, I put Lil Nigga down wit what we was trying to do and he was wit the whole thing.

Sahih finally made it up the Gardens and we put our plan together. Him and his brother was going to be in the rented F-150 Sahih got, and me and Lil Nigga was going to be in my Yukon. Shaheed gave me the AK; I had it laid out on my back seat. Plus, Lil Nigga had a 40 cal, which stayed on his lap.

We hit a lot of spots and was talking to all the major buls, who were running them blocks on our target areas. I was putting all the buls that dealt wit Saleem down on how he was out of the game, and that everything was going thru me now. Most of them agreed to deal wit me and a few others said they would talk to Saleem personally, before they did anything.

Now the only problems we ran into was them nigga's from McCaff Projects, the Fair Grounds Project, and them 3rd street niggas, because a lot of them didn't deal wit Saleem. It was just mainly words, but you could feel the tension in the air. It was a must that we get at them buls, before other niggas heard about how that they wasn't trying to go for the move we was trying to make.

After making our rounds, we all went back up to the Gardens.

"We got to get at them niggas tonight," I said.

"Yeah," Sahih agreed.

"Who we going to hit first?" Shaheed asked.

"I think me and Shaheed should hit McCaff first, just so we can scare their workers. Then we're going to go lay on the nigga Little E, who run that projects," said Sahih.

"Aight then, me and Lil Nigga going to do the same thing down 3rd Street, and I hope that I see that bitch ass youngbul out there. The one that kept saying that Peanut wasn't going for this shit. And after we shoot the block up, we're going to lay on Peanut too. I know exactly where his spot at," I told them.

Everybody went to gear up for tonight's mission. One thing about me and my boys, that was different from other niggas was, we don't have no problems putting that work in ourselves. Other niggas be trying to pay other mutha fuckas to do their dirty work. Don't get me wrong, we do the same thing, at times, but we put that work in also because some shit you just can't trust other niggas to do. I have seen a lot of good men go to the joint like that, and my Uncle always told me to keep my circle small and tight, and to be careful about who I send out to put some work in for me because everybody can't stand tall when them people be trying to give them life sentences and football numbers out.

Lil Nigga went out and stole two minivans for us. Shaheed got all the guns we needed for the mission, while Sahih went to grab all the masks and gloves.

It was 11:30 p.m. when everybody met up on Boyle St. Lil Nigga had the two stolen vans parked up in some abandoned houses' driveways, on the other side of Boyle St.

"Lil Nigga, which one is ours?" Shaheed asked.

"The all black Caravan right there."

"Come show me how to start it up and turn it off," Shaheed ordered.

They both walked over to the van. Meanwhile, Sahih was giving me everything I needed. Shaheed walked back over to Sahih's truck and came back with a duffle bag with an AK and a Mac 10 in it, and gave them to me. Lil Nigga and me also took two 40 cal's wit us.

After discussing our plans, we all went our different ways.

I followed Lil Nigga in my truck down to the Memorial Park. Parked my truck on a side street, then got in the van wit him. I laid out the plan to him again.

"Look cuz, I want you to just ride past the block, so we can see where everybody is, then, we're going to park so we can walk around and hit them niggas up. Now when we get back in the van I want you to ride back past there."

"Aight, I'm wit that," said Lil Nigga.

He rode past the block, and all of them niggas was out there talking in front of the bar.

"Lil Nigga, park in that alleyway right in back of the bar, so nobody will notice us running out wit these big ass guns."

We walked slowly down the alleyway and as soon as we hit the corner we both ran and started shooting. A few of them got away from us. After emptying our clips on the ones we caught, we ran back around to the van. Lil Nigga jumped in the driver seat. While he was pulling off, I pulled the clip out of the AK. I had two clips taped together upside down, then rolled my window down when Lil Nigga pulled in front of the bar. It was like five niggas over top of the ones we just shot-up. Boom, boom the AK was spitting rapid fire. Three of them dropped and the other two tried to run, but I kept shooting and another one fell.

Lil Nigga hit the gas when he heard sirens blaring in the distance. We hurried up and made it to my truck parked on the side street. I jumped in it and left the guns and the van with Lil Nigga. He took the gasoline he had in there and burnt the van up, then jumped in the truck with me.

Now, we were on our way to lay on the nigga Peanut. He didn't live to far from 3rd Street. I was hoping he'd be out there when we shot them niggas up. Peanut lived with his girl on a side street down Trainer, which is down the street and around the corner from 3rd. We knew each other real well. He was fucking this girl named Teefa that I was hitting around the same time as him.

She was a nice little petite light skin girl from up Upland. Teefa used to run and tell me everything the bul use to say about me. I had to check him one day, and he started bitching up, saying that the bitch was lying on him, because he didn't want to fuck her no more. I gave the nigga a pass, but after that little problem we had, he always had that certain look about him. He would speak, but you could tell that he didn't like me.

♦　　♦　　♦

Sahih and Shaheed went over McCaff and hit the block up and killed 2 people. They was now laying on Little E up the street from the bar that he be in every night playing pool. They been waiting for like an hour by the time Lil E came out of the bar and got into his car. He rode one block over to the Mobil gas station. Sahih pulled around the corner in an alleyway. Shaheed jumped out of the F-150, and ran up the alleyway and hid behind a dumpster waiting for Lil E to come out of the store. Lil E made his way out of the gas station with his head down, talking on a cell phone. Shaheed waited until he got to his car, before he ran up and shot Lil E twice in the chest and when he fell, Shaheed shot him twice in the head, just to make sure that he was dead. Shaheed ran back down the street, jumped in the truck wit Sahih and they were gone.

♦　　♦　　♦

Lil Nigga and me was parked down the street from Peanut's house. We sat out there for like an hour, waiting to see if he would come out, after he heard about what happened down at the bar with his homies. When he didn't come out, I rode past his house and seen the lights on. Also, while we was sitting out in the truck waiting on him, I kept seeing junkies go to the back of his house. I told Lil Nigga "I think this bul is serving these junkies from the back of the house!"

"I was thinking the same thing myself," said Lil Nigga.

"Well, won't you go see what's going on back there," I told him.

"I'll go back there, but what if he ain't serving people back there?"

"Then bring your ass back to the truck, and we'll call it a night."

"Aight. Give me your gun, just in case I run into some trouble back there."

"Let me pull around the corner, first, so I can let you out. We don't know who's looking out these windows. I'm going to be parked right down here at the end of the block, under the tree. Lil Nigga, be careful back there and make sure it's him, before you start gunning, aight?"

"Yeah, I got you cuz."

Lil Nigga jumped out of the truck. Like 5 minutes passed before I heard like 10 shots. I looked in my rear view mirror and saw Lil Nigga running down the street.

"Ae cuz, hurry up and pull off," He said jumping into the truck.

I pulled off at a nice pace. As I did, I saw the cop's lights flashing off of the walls of the houses.

"Oh shit cuz, they might have seen me jump in the truck. Hurry up and pull off!"

"Chill man you drawing. Calm the fuck down," I told him.

That's when police came flying past us. It was three cop cars back to back.

"Ae Lil Nigga, don't be drawing like that when police around," I barked.

"Naw cuz, I ain't bitching or nothing. It's just that I thought somebody probably seen me get in the truck," Lil Nigga responded.

"Naw, we cool, ain't nobody see you get in the truck. I was parked under a tree and it was nothing but abandon houses, in that area. So, what happened back there?"

"When I was walking down the street, I saw the junkie bul. I asked him where the work was at, because I heard somebody was selling it out their house around here. He was like 'Yeah, Peanut opened a house around here.' So, when I was following the junkie to the house, I asked him do Peanut serve you himself, or does he have a worker wit him? He told me, 'He had a worker wit him' and that 'Peanut was just in there to make sure nobody robs the spot.' When he told me that, I knew Peanut was the one carrying the gun. Anyway though, we get to the back door of the house, and the junkie knocks. I stand a little to the side, just in case Peanut looked out of the door. Instead a worker looked out, and seen it was a junkie. When he opened the door, the junkie walked in first and I walked in behind him. I saw Peanut sitting at the kitchen table wit a gun on it. Soon as he looked up I had my gun in his face and I shot him twice in the chest. That's when I heard the worker running behind me. He must of grabbed the gun off the table because he didn't shoot, until I was out of the yard. He shot at me I think two times and I shot back like eight times, I think. I didn't hit him though," Lil Nigga finally ended.

"Did he see your face?" I asked.

"Naw, I had my hood and hat pulled down low. That nigga Peanut is dead."

"Yeah, we got our man. Now, let's go on and get rid of these fucking clothes and gun..."

Chapter 21

Lil Nigga dropped me off last night down Delaware, after we got rid of the clothes and guns. When I got in, Mira woke up. She was horny and missing me, and even though I was tired I couldn't just roll over and go to sleep on her. We were fucking all through the night. When we both finally went to sleep, it was like six in the morning.

Shortly after, Aziz jumped in the bed wanting to play. Mira got up and made some food for us, while I stayed in the room wit Aziz watching 106th and Park. Aziz liked seeing them girls. I had to keep putting my hands in his face to get his attention off of them.

My boy was getting big by the day. I can't wait until him and his brother get big enough to start playing sports. Aziz already loves playing basketball on the little court I bought him. Tarik, I know for sure, is going to be a boxer. At the age of one, all he wants to do is fight.

"Nieem, come on down here and bring Aziz with you," Mira called.

I grabbed little Aziz and we headed down stairs to eat. Mira cooked some fried potatoes and eggs, with jelly and toast.

"Nieem, I forgot to tell you about the bul from up the Fairgrounds. I was at my mom house and my friend Keya started talking about her boyfriend and about how he be doing this and that for her. You know how girls get when a nigga got them all open and shit. Well anyway, she started talking about how they counted out seventy-five thousand in his house up in the Fairground."

"I didn't know he live up in the Fairground?" I said with my radar popping up.

"No, they live somewhere in Delaware, but you know she ain't going to tell me where. I used to always ask her, but she said that he told her don't bring or tell nobody where they live. Probably, he told her that because I fuck with you and he know you be on some crazy shit," Mira answered.

"We got to find out where they stay. I need that paper."

"I know, that's why as soon as she started talking about the money, I started asking a lot of questions."

"Did she notice it and asked anything like why you want to know this or that?"

"No, she was just running her mouth trying to brag about that lame ass, fat and out of shape nigga. She was trying to prove to me that he had some money, because I used to always tell her that he was running around faking like he was getting it."

"Shit, he got seventy-five thousand in the spot. The nigga can't be doing too much faking."

"Yeah, you right. That's why I said to myself, my baby need that and that fat ass nigga too soft to be running around here with all that money," said Mira.

"Are you going to see Keya today?"

"Yeah, she always comes over my mom house."

"Don't ask her shit else. Call me tonight when she gets to your mom house."

"Aight," said Mira.

After, she told me all of that my mind was racing, because this was the same bul that wasn't trying to deal wit us. The bul name is Black and he drives an all green Range Rover. I heard thru the streets that he had a connect up in New York wit some major Arabs that sold Heroin. I already knew he was getting money, but Mira ain't really deep in the streets like that to know. She think that if a nigga ain't fucking wit my squad, or my uncle Saleem, the nigga ain't holding. Sahih and Shaheed been wanting to get at this bul for a minute, because he used to hate on them to this chick that him and Sahih use to fuck. Sahih is going to be happy as shit when I tell him the news.

"Nieem, don't hurt my friend Keya, please," Mira said. "I love her a whole lot. We've been friends for years, and it's just that his black fat ass been hitting on her the whole time. So, if he's broke and can't support her no more, maybe she will leave his ass," Mira added.

"You crazy as shit. You better stay out of people's business."

"I do stay out of people's business. It's just that she always comes crying to me when he be beating her ass. I be wanting to call you, but I know you ain't wit that shit."

"Yeah, you right. She need to call her brother, or cousin or something."

After, Aziz took a nap, me and Mira got in the shower together and was fucking like crazy, for like a hour, then I got out of the shower and got dressed. By the time, Mira got out I was getting ready to leave.

"Nieem, I'm going to the market. Do you want anything special? Plus, give me some money because I don't have enough to get everything."

"Go in Aziz room and look in his Timbs box. I just put twenty thousand in there last week. And just make sure you grab some extra grapes for me. You know how you be complaining about me eating them all up."

"Aight," said Mira.

"Come here and give me a kiss. I'm about to leave."

We kissed, and then I headed out the door.

◆　◆　◆

Jumping on the highway on my way up to the city, I thought to myself, I'm going to have to be extra careful out here today. Word travels fast in Chester, because it's so small. Mutha fuckas' probably already know that we did that shit last night. When I got off the Highland Ave. exit, my phone went off. I saw it was Evon.

"What's up?"

"You just coming out?" She inquired.

"Yeah, I saw you left a couple of messages on my phone this morning, you alright?"

"I'm good; I just need some money to go shopping."

"You know where it's at. Go ahead and grab it," I said.

"I didn't know if you had to do something wit it or not."

"Naw, go ahead and take what you need."

"I thought you was staying here last night."

"I was but something had came up."

"Lil Nigga came past here earlier; he said to check on me. You better tell him stop showing up around here like that before he find out what he looking for," Evon rambled on.

"And what is he looking for?"

"For a nigga to be in here. Sike naw. You know I love my baby more than anything. Ya son keep asking for you, too. Please come and see him today, before I whip his ass."

"What 'cha going to whip his ass for?"

"Because he is getting into everything. I got Lil Hass over here, too, and them two together is a got damn handful. If they ain't fighting each other, they are tearing the damn house apart."

"Did you go check on the house up in Philly yet?" I asked.

"Yeah, they said in two months I could move in there and that I need eighteen hundred," she shot back.

"Go give them people that money today, so you can show them that you are really interested in the house. Call me when you get finished doing what you got to do for the day. Did my peoples take anything out of the house wit him?"

"No, he was trying to take Tarik and Lil Hass to the store wit him but I wouldn't let him."

"Why?"

"Because his little crazy ass stay in too much shit. He's not going to get my son and nephew killed in no shoot-out."

"I'm going to get wit you later on. I love you."

"I love you too, and make sure you find your way to my home tonight, or else I will come looking for your ass nigga."

"Aight."

When I got finished talking to Evon on the phone, I was already parked on Boyle St.

Lil Nigga and Shaheed was out there. Lil Nigga had started walking towards my truck. "Cuz, I see you pulled the Yukon out today," he said hopping in. "I just might have to go grab me a Cadi, instead of that Navi because this mutha fucka nice."

"What's up wit you cuz? How long you been out here today?" I asked.

"I opened the block up like 8 o'clock this morning. Only like 2,500 came so far. It's still 12 o'clock though. Did you see the paper today?" Lil Nigga asked.

"Naw," I answered.

"We killed 2 people down the bar, Peanut and a junkie is dead. Sahih and Shaheed killed 2 people around McCaffe and Lil E got killed at the Mobil gas station last night," Lil Nigga informed.

"Y'all strapped out here?" I asked.

"Yeah, we strapped. I got an AK in the grass in that yard me and Shaheed is sitting in," he answered.

I rolled down the window and called Shaheed.

"Lil Nigga get ya little ass in the back. You know I'm too fucking big to be sitting in the back of this truck," Shaheed said jokingly, but serious.

Lil Nigga got in the back of the truck.

"Nieem, what's good wit you? You read the paper today?" Shaheed asked.

"Naw, but Lil Nigga put me down on everything it was saying."

"I talked to Sahih earlier and he told me if we needed him, to call, because he was chilling for the day."

"Shaheed, you know that bul Black Regg?" I asked.

"Yeah, that's the nigga from yesterday. The one who was on some bullshit. He ain't trying to fuck wit us."

"Yeah, him. Mira just told me that he fuck wit the babe Keya she be wit."

"I use to fuck the shit out of Keya, before I went to jail. I haven't seen her ass yet.... And I was looking for her too," Lil Nigga chipped in.

"Well, the bul Black Regg wife'd her and he got her all open right now, so I don't think you're going to be getting any of that pussy yet. Anyway though, he counted out seventy-five thousand in a house in the projects with her. Then he made her take it down their house in Delaware. We are either going to follow her home tonight and grab her or we can wait for him to come home and just hit him up outside of the house," I told them.

"I just want to hit the bul up and bounce, although we could grab her and take the money too. But then we are going to have to kill her because we are definitely going to kill him," said Shaheed.

"Naw, man, we can't kill her. That's my baby right there." Lil Nigga said with much emphasis.

"Look, I already told Mira that nothing was going to happen to her. She love that girl to death. They knew each other since they were little. Mira only told me about him because of the money. She wanted me to go get that. She don't know that we was already trying to kill the bitch ass nigga."

"We got to get him tonight then, before he try and get us. I know he heard about all that shit that happened last night," said Shaheed.

"Mira is going to call me before she leaves to go home tonight."

"Oh yeah, I holla'd at Kasul today, too. I seen him over the Eastside, on the block. He was telling me that he heard about that shit that we did," said Shaheed.

"You told him we did that shit?" I asked.

"Ae, Nieem, you know I ain't slipping like that. He put two and two together. Just like we would have if a couple of bodies dropped over the Eastside. Everybody knows who the killers are in the city. Anyway though, he told me that he ran into some trouble wit them Crosby Square niggas and them Spanish niggas over there that sell that heroin, and he said them buls is trying to say fuck him," Shaheed said further.

"So, what is he going to do about it?"

"He didn't tell me anything. He just said that he was going to get at them niggas quick. Plus he said he was getting a lot of calls from them niggas down 3rd Street. They was asking him for some help, but he told them that he wasn't fucking wit them and that he was riding wit us. So, they either get down or lay down," Shaheed ended.

We all continued just talking and bullshitting. Then, we all decided to go grab something to eat. I drove all the way out to the Granite Run Mall just to go get some Chick-Fila. We sat in there and ate, then walked around the mall, going into different stores. I stopped by a store that sold DVD's and grabbed a couple of them. Lil Nigga wanted to go past Foot Locker, so he could grab some Timbs. As we were walking in the store, I see the nigga P at the counter. He was there by himself. P was one of the buls from over McCaff that get money and was under the bul Lil E. He sold heroin and powder. Soon as Shaheed seen him, he walked in back of him, and when P turned around all he saw was Big Shaheed in his face wit the brick on.

"P what's up? You ready to get down on the team?"

"I was trying to get one of y'all's number earlier. The only reason I said no yesterday was because of Lil E. I couldn't go against him. But he's gone, so I'm riding wit y'all now," P said nervously.

"Come thru the Gardens tomorrow, around noon, and we all are going to talk," Shaheed said aggressively.

"Shaheed I don't want no trouble. I'm just trying to get some money and feed my family I don't want no gun play or nothing," P pleaded.

"Yeah, I know, that's why I'm inviting you to my block, so niggas can know that you fuck wit us and that if they got a problem wit you, they got a problem wit us. Now, if I wanted to do something to you, I could have just waited for you outside in the parking lot, and blew ya fucking head off. You feel me?" said Shaheed.

"I feel you. I'll be over there tomorrow," said P.

He left the store scared as shit. The nigga was shaking and everything.

"Nieem, you see how much of a bitch that nigga is? P know we killed his man last night," said Shaheed.

"Yeah, ain't no way in hell I would have even agreed to do business with niggas that killed my man. Even if I was one man against a group of niggas. I would have put thirty thousand on all y'all nigga's head and laid back until you niggas got killed. Niggas be so scared that they can't even think and try to plan some shit out," I told them.

"Do y'all think we can trust him? The nigga P stabbed a nigga trying to play him in the joint," said Lil Nigga.

"That nigga ain't in jail no more. We play with them big ass guns out here. Ain't no mutha fucka playing with no knives. Plus, he probably did it under pressure. He know in jail you can't let shit slide. Out here on the streets most niggas that is getting money is soft. So he is going to be smarter than Lil E was and just go along wit us," said Shaheed.

Lil Nigga grabbed his Timbs and we was out of the mall. Back up the way, Evon called me as soon as we pulled into the Gardens.

"What's up, baby," I answered.

"Nothing, were you at?" said Evon.

"I just pulled up in the Gardens. Why, what's up?"

"I just wanted to see you that's all. I got something for you, too." Evon said seeming to have something up her sleeve.

"What you got for me?" I asked, playing into her game.

"Come around here and find out," she stated, a bit sensually.

"I'll be around there in a little while. I got to take care of a couple of things first, and I might need you to do some shit for me."

"I'm about to go around my sister house. So, if you need me that's where I will be." said Evon.

"Did you take the money to the people yet?"

"The house people?" she asked.

"Yeah."

"Oh yeah, I took it to them after I got off the phone wit you."

"Who name you put the house in?" I asked.

"Who else's? Mine nigga." Evon said with a small laugh.

"Naw, I thought we was going to put it in your sister's name, just in case police start fucking wit us."

"Nigga, I don't sell drugs. I do hair in a shop that I paid for with a loan I got from the bank," She countered.

"A loan that I'm paying," I corrected her.

"So, nobody else knows that."

"We hope nobody knows that, but what if I need to lay low. I can't stay there when shit get hot for me, because the house is in your name."

"Boy, shut up, ain't no police fucking wit us."

"Aight, keep on thinking shit sweet."

"Nieem, I love you."

"I love you too."

"I hope to see you tonight, too. I bought something special for you."

"What?"

"You'll see when you get home." Evon said with a bit sexiness.

"Aight then, I'm going to get wit you in little bit. I got to take care of something."

"Aight, I love you. Bye baby."

After I hung up the phone wit Evon, we got out of my truck and walked over to my young girl house where the stash was. Lil Nigga went inside to go grab the AK. He laid it in the grass. The block was still moving when we left. The youngbul that was working out there came over and handed Lil Nigga a stack and then walked back across the street to serve a customer. We stayed out there until like 10:30 p.m., that's when Mira called me.

"Hello," I answered, happy to hear my baby's voice.

"Hey baby," said Mira.

"What's up baby girl?"

"Nothing I was just calling to tell you I was going in for the night."

"How is my boy doing?" I asked.

"He right here playing on that basketball court, driving us crazy because he won't let us quit playing," said Mira.

"Who all in the house wit you?"

"My mom, my sister and Keya. Everybody about to leave though."

"Aight, I'll be home early tonight."

"Okay, what did you eat?" She asked.

"Nothing yet."

"My mom cooked, I'm going to bring you a plate."

"Aight."

"I love you and be careful out there. I'll see you when you get in tonight."

"I love you too baby. Don't wait up for me though."

"Why?" Mira asked.

"Because, I don't know how long I'm going to be out."

"Oh, I thought that meant you wasn't coming home tonight. Well, I'm going to let you go baby, bye." said Mira.

"I love you."

After the phone call, I called Shaheed over and told him, "come on man, hurry up, so we can follow her home."

"Aight, come on then."

We hurried up and jumped in the truck, I told Lil Nigga to stay out there and get some money, while we go take care of business. I never told him we was going down DE to go kill the bul Black Regg.

Shaheed drove up to Chester Township where my girl mom lived. We sat out there for like 15 minutes. That's when I saw my beautiful wife to be, getting into her new Lexus truck, which we traded her X5 for. She liked it better, too.

Everybody followed her out of the house. Keya got into a tinted up silver Volvo. It looked like it was brand new. It still had the temporary stickers in the car back window. When Shaheed saw Keya he said, "got damn. Keya bad as shit. I like her little light skin ass... I might have to step on Lil Nigga toes. Sike, naw but I'm definitely going to ask him for the okay to holla at the chick."

"Man, that's why I didn't bring Lil Nigga wit us, because the bitch would have fucked his judgment up."

"Damn Ock, how the hell did Black Regg pull her? I definitely won't be able to shoot her pretty ass. Look at her, with that pretty ass mink on. I could do some big things wit her. Plus, she smart because she wouldn't tell her best friend where she lived. She trained like a mutha fucka," Shaheed ended.

"Yeah, she definitely is, but she ain't that smart. The bitch still was running her mouth about the paper."

"You right," Shaheed countered.

Now, Keya definitely was a bad chick. She was 5'5", around 130 pounds. All her weight, it looked like, was in her ass. She had hazel eyes with shoulder length, jet black hair. While me and Shaheed was going back and forth, Keya was sitting in her car warming it up. She pulled up alongside Mira's truck and said something to her, then pulled off, hitting the horn twice. We waited until she got at the bottom of the street, before we pulled off to follow.

Shaheed was good at following people, so I didn't have to coach him. We usually would use two or three cars, just in case the person noticed he was being followed, but since it was a girl, she wouldn't be on point like a hustler would, I figured.

This was always one of my worst fears, that somebody would grab one of my baby moms, or my mom and sisters. I don't know what the hell I would do. Definitely I'd pay anything they wanted, and then try to kill them mutha fucka's later, if I found out who done it. But, nowadays niggas playing for keeps. If niggas grab you, best believe they are going to kill you.

Keya got straight on the highway heading to DE, with no idea that we were following her, but she was driving fast.

"Ae, Nieem the nigga must of told her to drive like this," Shaheed spoke up.

"Yeah, I tell Mira the same thing but I tell her to take a different route to the house every time."

Keya got off at the Delaware Avenue exit, on the Westside.

"Shaheed, slow up, because this exit right here got a traffic light at the bottom and I can see that it's red. So, just slow roll and try not to pull on the side of her," I told him.

"Ae, Nieem, I got this."

Keya pulled off, made a right and drove all the way up to Union Street; she parked in front of a nice row house. We pulled over down the street and watched her get a couple of things out of the car, before heading inside.

"Nieem, what time is it?"

"11:15 p.m."

"You think this a good place to kill the bul?" Shaheed asked skeptically.

"We cool. You see how dark it is out here. Ain't no mask in here?" I asked.

"Naw, we ain't got shit in here," Shaheed shot back, while keeping his focus on the house.

"I'm going to wrap my t-shirt around my face," I told him.

"I'm going to stay parked here, and signal you when he pulls up... You got your Nextel don't you?" Shaheed asked.

"Yeah."

"Aight then, put it on vibrate and the volume on low, so when I see his car pull up I can chirp you."

"It's 11:30 p.m. I'm only staying out there until like 1:30, and then it's your turn to lay on him," I made clear.

"Aight, that's cool."

Before I got out, I covered the bottom of my face with a black t-shirt. If somebody seen my face covered like this, they wouldn't pay any attention to it. They would think it was a scarf, because of the cold. When I got to Keya house, the only lights that shone were upstairs. I walked up on the porch and acted like I was knocking on the door, just in case somebody was looking out of the window, then I went and laid on the side of the porch.

It wasn't until 12:30 a.m. when I heard Shaheed come across the Nextel chirp.

"He parking out front now."

I pulled the 9mm, then rolled over and got on my knees.

When Black Regg stepped on the porch I jumped up wit the gun aimed in his face. He froze at the sight of the gun. That's when I told him to open the door, and don't try no crazy shit and I wouldn't kill him.

"All I want is the money and I'm gone." Were my last words.

"Please don't kill me. I got one hundred thousand in the house," Black Regg pleaded.

I stood a distance, because he was a big mutha fucka and I didn't want him to try and grab the gun from me. Black Regg opened the door and walked slowly into the dark house and then tried to run. I took off behind him, bop, bop, bop, bop, I start firing. The kitchen was as far, as he made it, before he dropped. I then ran over and shot him twice in the head to make sure he was gone.

As I'm running back towards the door, I hear Keya screaming. When I looked up at the top of the stairs, all I seen was her pointing a gun, bop, bop, she fired. I ran out of the door, un-phased by both shots. When I got back to the truck, Shaheed looked at me like I was crazy.

"Hurry up and pull off. Hurry up!!"

Shaheed peeled out of there.

"What happened? I didn't hear no shot's."

"Because, I took him in the house to kill him."

"Why?" he asked.

"Because, it was easier, and if I would have hit him on his porch, somebody probably would have seen."

"You alright? Where was Keya?"

"That bitch was upstairs when I shot him, but on my way out the bitch start shooting at me."

"Did she see it was you?"

"Naw, it happened too fast, but she could have killed me, if she would have just start shooting from the beginning."

We made it to my house safely. Shaheed waited for me to take off all of my clothes, so that he could burn them. I told him to come pick me up tomorrow, because my Yukon was parked up on the block and my truck was parked in back of my mom house. Shaheed left without a response.

Mira was upstairs on the phone with Keya, just like I expected. Keya asked her to come over, because she was scared, and that the police were there and she needed somebody to comfort her, after what just happened.

As soon as she got off the phone, I heard it from her.

"Nieem, why y'all had to kill him? Damn, it wasn't supposed to go down that way!" She shouted.

"Ae Mira, calm the fuck down... Y'all ain't do shit. We didn't even get a chance to follow her. She lost us on the highway."

"Well, who the fuck did this shit?"

"How the fuck would I know. I'm sitting here wit you."

"She asked me was you in the house."

"And what did you say?"

"What the fuck you think I said nigga? I ain't stupid. I told her you was in the bed sleep."

"Did she sound like she believed you?"

"You know she believed me, Nieem. That's my best friend."

"Well, you need to go see how your friend is doing."

"I'm going to take your truck alright?"

"I left it up the way."

"Why?"

"Because the police was out and I had a gun under the seat. I didn't want to take a chance of getting pulled over."

"Aziz in our bed sleep... Ya food is in the microwave. I'll be back. Give me a kiss.

I'm, sorry for getting mad at you. I just know how y'all crazy mutha fucka's is."

"Yeah, whatever. Best believe if that was my work, I would have killed Keya ass too."

"My best friend Nieem? That's crazy."

Mira left and went to console her friend. I'm glad, because I wanted to know if she seen the truck leave the scene, because we had to ride past the house to get off of the street.

Chapter 22

Six months done past, since I ran in the house and killed Black Regg. Which allowed us to take control of the Fair Grounds Projects. It took some time but everything was looking good. We started serving everybody on the Westside of Chester, while Kasul had the Eastside and he managed to get rid of them Ricans and all the other problems he had trying to take over the Eastside.

C even made out good, getting the two murders of the cops thrown out at the preliminary, but C went to trial on a tampering with a witness charge, and got a hung jury. The only thing they had for evidence was the wire that Lil Don had on.

C been home going on three months now. Him and Lil Nigga was hanging real hard. Lil Nigga went and grabbed an all black Range Rover and moved his girl into a condo down on Delaware Ave. in Philly. He was doing good for himself. Plus, him and C was robbing niggas that his old celly from Philly turned him on too. They was getting a lot of money off of them robberies.

Sahih and Shaheed were getting money as usual. They was trying to stay low key now, because our names were ringing bells. They sold all of their cars and bikes, and stopped wearing jewelry. All they were doing was stacking paper and spending time wit their kids.

Me, I was doing the same thing. I sold my two trucks and bought a 2001 F-150 and a 2001 Crown Vic. My Uncle told me to let Lil Nigga start serving everybody, so that I could stay off the scene for a while, but I didn't listen to him. I was serving any and everybody. Well, I'm not going to say anybody, because most of the people I was serving, Saleem was serving them before. It was just that he didn't trust them no more because people was only dealing wit me because they was scared. He told me that the first chance they got to get me off of the scene; they would go straight for it. Saleem was talking about the police when he said that, because they were the only people that could get us off the scene.

Everything was going well with my two boys. I was trying to keep them together. Mira just graduated from a computer school and was trying to find a job in that field. We still lived in Delaware, but had plans on moving, after we got married next year.

Mira stayed on my ass about getting out of the dope game and moving down south to Georgia, by her family. She also kept trying to convince me to start buying property and investing money in legitimate things. Mira always says, "Nieem, there's only two ways out of the game. Either dead or in jail." And I knew that, but the dope game was all I had. Also, I know buls that actually made it in the game. My Uncle was one of them. He was in his late 40's and still getting money behind the scenes and that's how I want to be. I looked up to Saleem. He was my hero and everything he did I wanted to do. Plus, my Uncle gave me full control over all of his business now, so I couldn't just up and leave like that.

Now, Evon on the other hand, was also doing good for herself. She was going to school right now to get her cosmetology license. Tarik and her were now living in Philly. She still got mad when I wasn't up there wit them. I never told her that I was going to get married to Mira. She probably will go crazy and try to kill my ass. All in all I loved her, even though I didn't always show it half of the time.

Chapter 23

It was a sunny June morning. I was leaving from Evon's house in Philly and headed up the Gardens to check on Lil Nigga and the rest of my youngbuls. Evon's house was only 20 minutes away from my block. I pulled up and everything was looking good. I saw the dope fiends lined up trying to get served. Sahih and Shaheed was sitting in the yard across the street. They had brought the house, so that we all could just chill and fuck the young girls around the way in it. Nobody was allowed to have drugs stashed in there.

When I got out of the car, Sahih and Shaheed called me over. I told Lil Nigga that I would holla at him as soon I was done.

"Nieem, we got a big problem," Sahih spoke up.

"What?" I asked.

"You know Bruce and Mack?"

"Yeah, the two cousins up there on Swartz street. They be getting work off of us."

"Well, Mack little brother got locked up wit his gun, and the gun came back to my cousin Jane, because the dick heads ain't scratch the numbers off."

"What the fuck is she doing buying them guns period?" I asked a bit heated.

"That's what I asked her. She was only suppose to do it for Shaheed, and nobody else.

She went behind his back and was selling a lot of people up here in the hood guns."

"So how is there a big problem? Youngbul got to go ahead and do the little time he going to get," I told them.

"The big problem is that she told on me. Jane got indicted yesterday and told on me, Bruce and Mack. Now, I already talked to her. I told her it was cool to tell on me because I can only get like 2-3 years for a gun anyway. It ain't like I'm looking at some hell'a time. I already talked to the lawyer and everything... My concern is them other two niggas... Them niggas been locked up so many times. I know that they ain't trying to go back to jail," said Shaheed.

"So did y'all holla at them yet?"

"Naw, we been looking for them all morning. The A.T.F. ran in their house today, too. Everybody up the way been talking about it. So, they probably laying low somewhere, but we got to get at them niggas quick," Shaheed said with much emphasis on the quick.

"Damn, that's a problem. A big fucking problem." I responded.

"Ain't no telling what them niggas will do to her," said Sahih.

"Yeah, that's a problem, too. But truthfully I was thinking about how them buls is going to try and line me up," I told him.

"Naw, Mack going to stand strong. You got to worry about that damn Bruce, though. He look like that type of slimy nigga," said Shaheed.

"Well, we'll see how this plays out, but we got to kill them two niggas to be on the safe side," I made clear.

"You right. We got to get on top of that, now," Sahih chipped in.

After the conversation wit them two, my mind was just racing. Ain't no telling what them buls would do. They could set us up wit the Feds or anything or try to kill my man's peoples. Shit crazy.

I walked across the street to holla at Lil Nigga. My cuz was a loyal nigga. After, we took over the Westside of the city, I gave him some blocks of his own and told him that he didn't have to run my block, but he said he would, because he didn't trust nobody else with my paper. Plus, he wanted me to stay low and out of the way.

"What's up Cuz?" I greeted.

"I can't call it," he shot back, with a dap of the fist.

"How the block doing out here today?"

"Only like a stack came so far."

"You heard about that shit that happened?" I asked.

"About Bruce and them?"

"Yeah."

"That shit is crazy. We went looking for them niggas already."

"Well, I need you and C to get on them niggas tops, because them niggas been getting coke from me and they might snitch on a nigga once they get grabbed by the Feds."

"Oh, I didn't know that it was that deep. I'm going to make it my business to get at them niggas," Lil Nigga said, reassuringly.

"I just wanted to put you down wit what was going on... I'm about to go take care of a couple things. I'm going to get wit you a little later," I told him.

I went back over to holla at Sahih and Shaheed and we all jumped in my truck to go look for Bruce and Mack. They had peoples on the Eastside, so we thought they'd probably be laying low over there. Shaheed also called Kasul up and told him that we was looking for them and if he seen them to call us.

After a couple hours, with no luck, we told Lil Nigga and C to go lay at Bruce and Mack's girls houses because nine times out of ten, that's where they were, or if not, their girls would lead us to them. I dropped Sahih and Shaheed off up the way and went down to Delaware. Suddenly, my phone rung I looked at the unfamiliar number clueless.

"Yoo," I answered.

"Hello, is this Nieem?"

"Yeah, who this?"

"This Keisha, Khalil's sister."

"Oh damn, my bad Keisha. I didn't recognize your voice. It's been awhile since I heard from you."

"Yeah, it has. Well, Khalil told me to call you because he got locked up last night for a shooting."

"Did the person die?"

"No, that's how Khalil got caught."

"How much is his bail?"

"His bail is a million dollars."

"Damn, they act like he killed the nigga."

"Yeah, I know. He told me to tell you that he would get the rest of that to you next week... I asked him what, but he said you would know what he's talking about and that to don't worry about trying to get him out on bail, because the Feds would be all over our asses. Plus, he said that he already got somebody on the bul top too; either pay him or you know."

"Oh, okay, I understand where he coming from... Do he need any lawyer money?"

"No, he already had a lawyer; he was paying monthly, just in case he got locked up for anything."

"What about commissary money?"

"He cool, I just put 500 on the books... One of his young boys gave him the money."

"Oh, okay then. Tell him to send me a kite or something, if he needs me for anything, and I mean anything. Tell him just like that for me Keisha, seriously."

"I will."

"Do you need anything?"

"No."

"You sure?"

"Yup."

"Well, just give me a call."

"Aight, I'll talk to you later Nieem, bye."

I hung up the phone wit Keisha and was fucked up over the news of my man Khalil getting locked up. I wonder who the hell he done shot up. He must be cool, though, because he said he didn't need my help. I know if it was real serious, he would have holla'ed at me from the gate. I know Khalil is a soldier, though. Ain't no doubt in my mind that he is going to stand strong. We have done a lot of shit together over the years.

Well, I guess I'm going to call it a night. I went in the house with my baby girl Mira and my son Aziz. I didn't come home last night, and she has been snapping about that shit, lately, because she knows about me staying wit Evon. Mira always tells me that when we get married, I got to completely leave Evon alone, or else there's no reason for us to get married, if she can't have me to herself. Everything she was saying was right, but I loved Evon, too, and I couldn't just get up and leave her like that.

Chapter 24

It was 10 o'clock in the morning when my phone rung, "What's up Ock?"

"Ae, Nieem where you at?" Sahih barked.

"I'm in the crib down Delaware," I said.

"Oh, okay, I thought you was up top. I was going to come past there on my way out the crib. Anyway though, you ain't going to believe what these pussies did last night," said Sahih.

"Who you talking about?"

"Bruce and Mack, them niggas killed my peoples. They caught her coming out of the house, going to work."

"What time was this?" I asked.

"Like around 10 o'clock." Sahih said with anger in his voice.

"Where the fuck was Lil Nigga and them?"

"They was on the block hustling, but they said they didn't see either one of them buls come past the block," Sahih shot back.

"Damn, I'm sorry to hear about ya peoples; that's fucked up."

"Yeah, me too. My family is going crazy right now. Plus, the Feds and everybody was up there today. Bruce and Mack was stupid as shit killing her. She was a fucking federal witness."

"That shit ain't cool. Don't worry, though, because I'm going to kill them bitch ass niggas... This just put the icing on the cake, you feel me?" I came back with.

"Yeah."

"What you about to do though?" I asked.

"I'm about to go up the way, around my peoples house. I told everybody to shut the block down for the day up there." He answered.

"Where Shaheed at?"

"He should be up there already."

"Aight then, I'm on my way. I'm going to hit the horn when I get in front of the house." I said.

"Aight." Sahih said, then disconnected.

Damn, that's fucked up they killed that man cousin. All hell going to break loose, now. They want to start killing family members. That is total disrespect, but if they want to play like that, then we can play like that. I got dressed and let Mira know about everything that had happened. I also told her to be on point because you never know what type of time them niggas was on.

On my way up to the city, I got a call from Shaheed. "What's up Ock?"

"Nieem, where you at?"

"On my way up the way," I told him.

"Naw, don't come up here yet. The Feds got this mutha fuckin' whole neighborhood surrounded, going door to door questioning people about Jane's murder," Shaheed informed.

"Yeah?"

"I'm in the bathroom, looking out the window. It's like a hundred cops out that bitch. No bull shit," Shaheed replied.

"All Feds?" I asked.

"Naw, Chester Police and Chester Homicide Detectives, the Feds and ATF," he answered.

"Oh, okay. I was about to say, ain't no way in hell that a hundred Feds was up there alone," I answered.

"Naw, hell no. I think they looking for Bruce and Mack, because word is that some youngbul seen them do it," Shaheed said further.

"Them niggas done. They ain't going to be able to get to that youngbul, after they just killed a witness. The Feds is going to hide him now," I said.

"Yeah, you right, but to make matters worse them mutha fuckas ran up in my girl house last night," said Shaheed.

"Who?" I said.

"A.T.F. They said I had a warrant for that gun shit."

"You already knew that was coming, though," I said.

"Yeah, I'm going to turn myself in later on. I don't want them thinking that I had something to do wit this. I was waiting, though. I wanted to see you and my brother first," Shaheed went on to say.

"Ya brother said he was on his way up there," I said.

"I know; he didn't get here yet."

"Well, Ockie, I'm not coming thru there if the police is all around that bitch."

"I'm going to call you later then, when they leave."

"Aight."

"Aight Ock."

Shit was getting crazier by the day. Sahih said that they might try some stupid shit like this. Them damn Feds are around here now. I definitely got to shut my block down, until shit blow over. I tried to call my cuz like four times. This nigga ain't even answering the damn phone. I cursed, all the while hoping he wasn't in one of them stash houses. The nigga might get scared and start flushing everything when he see them cops and shit. Fuck it, though.

I headed to go holla at Saleem. I haven't seen him since last week when he introduced me to the connect from down Texas.

We all went out to eat and Saleem let him know that I was taking over everything and that from now on he was no longer in the game.

Me and the connect got together the next day and discussed prices and made small talk on other things.

The connect was from Dallas, but had peoples that lived in Philly. Him and Saleem had been dealing wit each other for years. They got introduced to each other by a lady, who was the connects cousin. This was five years ago and they was dealing wit each other ever since.

His name is Fluco; A mix of Mexican and Black, but he looked more black than Mexican.

Fluco was going to give me 100 bricks, first to see how long I would take to move them, and after that, he would triple the order. Also, he would have them delivered to me the first time for free, but the next time he was going to charge a thousand dollars on each brick, on top of the price I was paying. I told him that I was going to start coming down there to get them myself, after the first hundred jawns, because it would be cheaper.

◆　　◆　　◆

Ameer's was crowded when I got there. I didn't park in the back, because we stopped doing business in the store. Plus, I wasn't driving any more of them Benzs and trucks. When I got inside Saleem was standing behind the counter talking to Amina. Saleem waved me over.

Amina was looking so beautiful in her all black, Louis Vuitton hijab, with the designs in white. She made sure I seen her pretty smile. I was just thinking about how her body would look without the hijab, knowing Amina had a body, because of seeing her before, when she wasn't garbed up.

"As-Salaam-Alaikum."

"Wa-Alaikum-As-Salaam, Nieem," they both said at the same time.

"How you been Amina?"

"Al-Hamdu-lilah, I'm tayiib," she replied.

"Amina, give me a few minutes and we'll finish our conversation about that issue you got," Saleem told her.

"Salaam-Alaikum. I'll see you later Nieem," she said then walked off.

"I'm going to be waiting for you, too," I told her.

"Nieem, what's up wit you? How you been?"

"I'm good. I was coming by to see how you was doing... Is she married yet?" I asked.

"No, why?"

"Because I been wanting Amina for the longest."

"Yeah, I see how you two be looking at each other. She ain't fooling with you, though, because you in the streets too hard. Amina already lost her Abu to these streets, that's why she's so cautious about who she vibes with. Plus, you don't even pray and she ain't going for that at all."

"Unc, how you know I don't pray?"

"I don't, but by your actions and the way you talk tells a whole lot about whether you pray or not... So, what happened wit that lady up there?"

"Bruce or Mack killed that lady over some bull shit guns. Now, the Feds and everybody is like a hundred deep, going door to door questioning people."

"You shut the block down?"

"Yeah, Shaheed or Sahih did."

"Did you get wit Fluco yet?"

"I got the first pack the other day. I wanted to know how you use to get the work from down there."

"I used all different type of ways to bring it up here. I'll explain it to you later. I don't like talking to much in here anymore, just to be on the safe side."

"I feel you."

While me and Unc was talking, I got a call from my sister Keisha.

"Where you at?"

"At the store wit Unc, why?" I asked sort of alarmed.

"Hurry up and get to Crozer; Mira and Lil Aziz just got into an accident. Aziz is the only one at the hospital, though. They said Mira didn't make it. She died at the accident scene."

"Stop bullshitting, Key," I told her. My heart nearly jumped out of my chest.

"I'm dead serious. Hurry up and go see what's up wit Aziz... Me and mommy is on our way there."

"Aight," I answered in a choked up voice, while tears escaped my eyes.

"Unc, I got to go to the hospital. Mira and Aziz got into an accident and Mira didn't make it but Aziz did. They sent him to Crozer Medical Center."

"Come on Nieem, I'm going wit you."

When we pulled up to the hospital it was so crowded out there, that the hospital security and police, wouldn't let nobody in except family. People was outside crying and everything. When me and Saleem started walking to the door, Mira's mom came rushing over, saying "My baby died Nieem. My baby died... Aziz is in there wit a collapsed lung and he got head injuries." She said through the cries.

"Who was all in the jeep?" I asked wiping away tears.

"Mira, Aziz, Rene and Ebony. Everybody else is alright except Mira and Aziz," her choked up voice carried on.

"Who hit them," I asked, 'I'm going to kill that mutha fucka for doing this shit,' I thought to myself.

"That mutha fucka from over the bridge. He was all drunk and high and ran a red light. He hit them on the passenger side. Her door came off and she flew out and hit her head on the ground and broke her back... Aziz flew out of the door also, because the door came off in the back too."

All I could do was hug her, asking Allah to give me strength. We went in the hospital and they let me see them working on my son. He was looking so helpless on that bed.

I felt bad that I wasn't there to protect him like a father was suppose to.

His face was bruised bad, and blood was everywhere. Still I remained strong for Ms. Robin, because she was going thru it, even more than me, at this point. Aziz was her first and only grandson.

The doctors told us we had to leave and that they were sending him to the Children's Hospital up in Philly.

"We fixed his collapsed lung," the doctor informed, "So right now, it looks like he is going to make it, but we are sending him to Philadelphia because that's the best hospital for kids. They can monitor him better and give him better care."

"Okay, thank you," said Ms. Robin.

Everybody was outside the hospital arguing and getting ready to fight, because the guy who hit Mira, family was out there. My whole squad was present as well. They just played the background though, seeing how fucked up I was. My dad had came by and I rode with him up to the hospital. Along the way we was talking about Mira, and how I loved her, and how I was mad about how she got killed. I slipped up and told him that if I ever seen the nigga that did this to my family, I was going to kill him. He acted like he didn't hear it and just started talking about something else.

At the hospital Evon was sitting in the hallway crying her heart out. My sister and other family was in attendance. Aziz was in surgery for a couple of hours, and then they took him to the intensive care unit, where me and my mom spent the night.

Chapter 25

For the past couple of days I was running back and forth from the hospital. Lil Nigga was taking care of everything else for me. Sahih, had came past the hospital and told me that the police had grabbed Bruce and Mack and charged them with tampering with a Federal Witness by Murder and that they was looking at the death penalty. He also said that Shaheed turned himself in to the A.T.F., and they charged him with straw purchasing of guns and he should be coming home next week on home monitoring.

I told Sahih that as soon as the nigga who killed my girl come home, I was going to kill him, on sight. Sahih kept trying to get me to use my head and be smart about it and to not let my emotions get involved. But how can I not.

Aziz didn't make it out of the hospital in time to make it to his mom's funeral. She looked so peaceful in her all white, in the casket. I wanted to jump in there and take her place. That's how much love I had for her, even though I didn't always show it.

Chapter 26

Shaheed still hadn't gotten out of jail. Me and Sahih was out late last night doing homework on this bul from over Middletown in the city. The nigga was getting money under our noses, but he wasn't getting no work from us or Kasul and them. We told Kasul about him and he gave us the green light.

Kasul couldn't do it because he was fucking the bul sister and the nigga knew Kasul and his peoples real good. It just so happened that he didn't come home last night. We sat out there until like 4 o'clock in the morning waiting to grab him.

I got in the house wit Evon around five in the morning. She was knocked out, in a deep sleep. It seemed like I just laid down when the phone started ringing. All I heard was my sister Key saying "hurry up, Nieem get out of there. Hurry up. The Feds is kicking in mommy door right now."

"Oh shit, aight."

I hung up the phone and was telling Evon that I was leaving because the Feds just ran in my mom house.

On my way out of the door, I looked out of the window and seen the Philly police blocking the street off, up near the corner. I ran to the back of the house and looked out the dining room window and saw that the street was blocked off. Ten seconds later I heard the banging on the door.

"Feds open up the door."

I ran back upstairs to Evon. Luckily, Tarik and Aziz wasn't in the house. "Damn, baby they coming to get me."

"Nieem, why did you grab that gun?" She asked while crying.

"E, I can't go out like that. I'm going out in a blaze of glory. They ain't taking me to jail."

"Nieem please, you don't even know what they coming for."

"I did too much shit in my life to sit here and chance it, E."

"Think about the boys Nieem."

The Feds was still messing around with the door. The phone start ringing, Evon picked it up, "Hello."

"Evon, this is the FBI out in front of your house. Tell Nieem to surrender and we won't kick the door in. We are going to give him five minutes. We know he's armed and dangerous, so we're coming in shooting."

"Please don't, I'll talk to him."

"Okay Evon, five minutes," They hung up the phone in her ear.

"Nieem, they said you got five minutes, or else they are coming in here shooting."

"Go lay in the tub in the bathroom and put a mattress over top of you and put a wet rag over your face, because they are going to start shooting gas in here."

"Please, Nieem, no."

"Get your ass in the bathroom before you get killed in here."

"No! I'm staying right here with you."

"Okay then sit your ass right there then."

I grabbed my AK, cocked it and was standing at the top of my steps. They kicked the door in and came bursting inside. I ran back to E and yelled to her, "Go lay in the fuckin tub."

"No... No..." Evon yelled when the Feds seen me at the steps.

Boom, boom, boom...That's all you heard was shots fired.

To be continued....

Street Dreamz Publications

NAME _____

ADDRESS _____

CITY _____ STATE _____ ZIP _____

Check the books you would like to order

     _____   The Life We Chose $14.95

     _____   The Life We Chose, Part 2 *(coming soon)* $14.95

     _____ Corporate Thug *(coming soon)* $14.95

              Total for books ordered $ _____

Shipping & Handling

How many books are you ordering?

First book - $3.95

Each *additional* book, add $1.00   +

     _____ x $1.00 = $____

     Total for Shipping & Handling $ _____

TOTAL ENCLOSED $ _____

This offer is subject to change without notice.

*Make Checks payable to **STREET DREAMZ PUBLICATIONS***

Send check or money order (no cash or CODs) to:
Street Dreamz Publications
P. O. Box 258
Chester, PA   19013

Thank you!

**For more information, please visit our website,
www.streetdreamzpublications.com**